"The author clearly knows her milieu and brings her characters and setting to life. There are a lot of natural suspects, [and] together with a good amount of misdirection, the result [is] a credible whodunit."

—*Mysterious Reviews*

"Readers get treated to the inside scoop of what happens at a popular soap opera offscreen as Eileen Davidson uses her experience on *The Young and the Restless* and *The Bold and the Beautiful* to create the background to this exciting, heady, and enthralling mystery. . . . With great characters, a fun look at soaping, and an engaging whodunit, fans beyond the soaps will enjoy this fine amateur sleuth tale."

—*Genre Go Round Reviews*

"Ms. Davidson is an actress, and clearly knows the inner workings of daytime dramas. She's great at giving the reader an inside look at the real-life soap behind the soap. . . . You'll find this to be a fast, frothy read. The author's breezy writing style really makes the whole caper fun, without going over the top."

—*CA Reviews*

"In this fast-paced and entertaining mystery that takes place on the set of a soap opera, *The Young and the Restless* star Davidson's heroine has an engaging voice laced with humor and irony. . . . This glimpse into the daytime television world is interesting and informative, and one need not be a soap fan to enjoy the well-plotted, suspenseful story."   —*Romantic Times*

Also by Eileen Davidson

Death in Daytime

Eileen Davidson

Dial Emmy
for
Murder

A SOAP OPERA MYSTERY

AN OBSIDIAN MYSTERY

OBSIDIAN
Published by New American Library, a division of
Penguin Group (USA) Inc., 375 Hudson Street,
New York, New York 10014, USA
Penguin Group (Canada), 90 Eglinton Avenue East, Suite 700, Toronto,
Ontario M4P 2Y3, Canada (a division of Pearson Penguin Canada Inc.)
Penguin Books Ltd., 80 Strand, London WC2R 0RL, England
Penguin Ireland, 25 St. Stephen's Green, Dublin 2,
Ireland (a division of Penguin Books Ltd.)
Penguin Group (Australia), 250 Camberwell Road, Camberwell, Victoria 3124,
Australia (a division of Pearson Australia Group Pty. Ltd.)
Penguin Books India Pvt. Ltd., 11 Community Centre, Panchsheel Park,
New Delhi - 110 017, India
Penguin Group (NZ), 67 Apollo Drive, Rosedale, North Shore 0632,
New Zealand (a division of Pearson New Zealand Ltd.)
Penguin Books (South Africa) (Pty.) Ltd., 24 Sturdee Avenue,
Rosebank, Johannesburg 2196, South Africa

Penguin Books Ltd., Registered Offices:
80 Strand, London WC2R 0RL, England

First published by Obsidian, an imprint of New American Library,
a division of Penguin Group (USA) Inc.

First Printing, June 2009
10 9 8 7 6 5 4 3

*I dedicate this book
to my mom, Charlotte Greathouse.
You are an amazing mother!*

ACKNOWLEDGMENTS

I acknowledge my husband, Vince Van Patten, and Annamarie Davidson for allowing me to torture them with ideas all the time. And to the terrific Marthayn Pelegrimas for her great eye and editing skills.

Chapter 1

"Alex! Alex! This way!"

"No, this way, Alex—your left!"

"Over here, Alex!"

"Great dress, Alexis. Who are you wearing?"

I exited the limo, making sure not to flash anyone. Just then a crowd of fans caught sight of me and burst into screams.

"Alex, we love you! We love you! Why did you leave *The Yearning Tide*?"

Why did I leave? How could I stay on that show when the entire cast and crew had believed that I murdered the head writer? Could you work with a bunch of people who thought you were capable of such a horrendous thing?

But now I worked on *The Bare and the Brazen* and it *was* a great gig. I played two characters, one of which looked completely different from myself! I had a prosthetic nose and false teeth (made by the same guy who did Austin Powers's). The hours were a little long sometimes because of the dual roles, but I was having a helluva good time. The primary character, Felicia Stewart, a psychiatrist, is the heroine of the show. She has a not-so-attractive twin sister, Fanny Stewart, who was given up for adoption and raised in the South. Fanny has bad teeth and an attitude to match. She's jealous of her sister and always up to no good. Fanny's the fun one to play, but then it's always more fun to be bad. Unfortunately that can be true in real life, too.

As I turned and smiled, I was assaulted by a multitude of flashbulbs exploding in my face. My manager, Connie, grabbed my elbow and steered me past the paparazzi.

"Al, *Entertainment Tonight* wants to talk to you—right up ahead."

"I can't, Connie." I felt a drop of sweat traveling from between my shoulder blades down to the small of my back.

"What do you mean, you can't? It's *ET*, for God's sake. Please just get over yourself and talk to them."

"Connie, you're on my train. I seriously mean I can't go talk to them." I gestured to the rear of my dress, and sure enough, Connie's spike-heeled Manolo Blahnik was pinning me to the red carpet.

"Oh! Sorry, doll." She moved off my dress and ushered me over to the *ET* reporter. "Jeez, it's gotta be a hundred degrees out here. Why is it always so damn hot at the Daytime Emmys? I'm dying." She dabbed at her bronze face.

"I know what you're saying, Con," I told my manager. "I feel like my face is melting."

"You look great, doll. Just do your thing!"

Mary Hart thrust a large microphone with the letters *ET* in my face.

"Alexis, thanks for talking with us. So, how does

it feel to be here tonight representing a different show?"

"It's great! I'm having so much fun. The cast and crew of *The Bare and the Brazen* are terrific. And you know, after all the drama of last year, it's nice to make a fresh start."

"We understand you'll be presenting Outstanding Supporting Actor with Jackson Masters. Now, there's a hunk!"

"Yes, I'm very excited about it. Jackson's a sweetheart."

"Thanks so much for talking to us, Alexis. You look amazing. Who are you wearing?"

I was dying to tell them I was wearing Vintage Chanel and diamonds by Van Cleef & Arpels. But before I could answer, the mike was quickly whisked away from my face and shoved into the more in-demand face of Ellen DeGeneres. "Ellen, you look amazing tonight. . . ."

Connie's gravelly voice cut through the wall of noise. "By the way, Al, the stage manager asked me if you'd seen Jackson. He never showed up for rehearsal."

"No, I haven't. But he always blows off rehearsals. He'll probably run up there at the last minute. He loves to jerk people's chains."

I proceeded up the steps to the Kodak Theatre and took a deep breath. Bells were ringing, letting everyone know the show was about to start.

"Please take your seats; we start in five minutes. Five minutes, everyone!" came blasting over the PA system.

The Kodak Theatre was a fairly new award venue and part of a very large and expensive attempt to overhaul Hollywood Boulevard. They had done a good job. There were various floors with bars, restaurants and shops connected to the theater.

I gingerly walked down the aisle, being careful not to trip on my train, and found my seat in the front row.

"Hi, Elmo!" Now, that was exciting. Elmo from *Sesame Street* was sitting in my row. Well, the great Kevin Clash and his alter ego, Elmo. I had to get a photo with the famous puppeteer. My five-year-old daughter, Sarah, would be thrilled.

"Hey, Alex." I looked over and saw Lisa Daley smiling at me from the *Yearning Tide* section.

"Hey, Lisa. How are you?" Lisa was one of the few people on *The Tide* who had remained my friend after I left the show. Some of the other actors, though, guiltily looked away. My feelings had been hurt when I learned how many people had thought I was capable of actually killing another human being. But I guess in hindsight I couldn't blame them, really. It had looked pretty bad.

The head writer had given me a very hard time, trying to get me written off the show. A shouting match started between us that was witnessed by, um, everyone in the production office. And then that same writer ended up bludgeoned to death with her Emmy. If the situation had been reversed, I probably would have thought the same thing.

"Take your seats, people. We're counting down to live television! One minute . . . one minute."

Chapter 2

The stage manager ran up to me in a panic, which is never good with one minute left.

"Ms. Peterson, could you please come backstage and get ready to present? Have you seen Mr. Masters?"

"No. You still haven't found him?"

I scanned the room. We were presenting the first award. This was cutting it close even for Jackson. I grabbed my train and hustled backstage into all the commotion. Hair and makeup sat me down in a chair facing a portable makeup station complete with fifteen blazing-hot lightbulbs. They gave me the once-over with powder and hairspray.

There was a mad dash as stragglers took their seats. As I moved to the wings, a sudden loud explosion of music enveloped the stage.

"Thirty seconds . . . twenty seconds. Ten, nine, eight, seven, six, five, four, three and we are live!"

I've often wondered why they bothered counting down when they never seemed to get to number one.

"Welcome to the thirty-ninth annual Daytime Emmy Awards, hosted by Rachael Ray and Jerry

Springer." Thunderous applause erupted for the two stars.

There must have been at least three thousand fans seated in the theater, and as Rachael and Jerry walked onto the stage, they burst into cheers and applause.

"Welcome," said Rachael. "Tonight is going to be an exciting evening, isn't it, Jerry?"

"Yes, Rachael, it is. And it's my pleasure to be hosting this illustrious event with someone as lovely and charming as you."

"Oh, thank you, Jerry. Looking out at the crowd, I see the finest in daytime television are here. All the talk shows, game shows, children's shows, cooking shows and, of course, *the* best of the best in daytime dramas are being represented."

"Well, then, let's get to it, Rachael."

"Yes, let's. Our first presenters are one hot couple. She's proven that forty really is the new twenty. And if that's true, then he's proof that twenty must be the new embryo. From *The Bare and the Brazen*, it's two-time Emmy winner Alexis Peterson and the gorgeous newcomer Jackson Masters."

Who wrote this stuff, anyway? I hesitated. More important, should I go on without Jackson or what? I looked at the stage manager questioningly for direction. The producer of the event, Dave Crane, ran up to me.

"Alexis! Just go without him. Make sure to read his part of the cue cards. Can you do that?"

"Yeah, Dave, of course. . . . I'll do my best."

I carefully walked out onto the top step of the epic staircase and into the mouth of this huge theater. An explosive burst of applause and screams greeted me from the balconies and arena seating, where all the fans were going wild. Without Jackson to lean on for support, I knew it would take every fiber of my being not to trip on my train as I tried to make it down twelve perilous steps to finally get to the stage. I took my time as I cautiously felt my way down the stairs, smiling and looking as if I did this in four-inch heels every day of my life. Why did I wear this stupid dress with this stupid train? Oh, yeah: it was worth ten thousand dollars. And it was free.

I took the last step. I made it. I sighed with relief as I approached the microphone that was poking out of the stage floor.

"Good evening. I'm here to present the award for Outstanding Supporting Actor in a Drama Series." I looked behind me one last time. No Jackson. "Unfortunately, my costar is nowhere to be found! Probably somewhere doing push-ups, ha-ha! You think he was born with that six-pack?" Not so great but the best I could come up with on the spur of the moment. Give me a break! I was thinking on my feet. I quickly looked at the next cue card and read Jackson's lines.

"The nominees for Outstanding Supporting Actor in a Drama Series are . . . Jamie Martin, *The Best Days Are Ahead*." I paused as they ran a quick clip of each actor's work. "Thad Weber, *The Depths of the Sea*. Don Duncan, *The Tears of Tomorrow*. Roman Stroud, *The Yearning Tide*. Vance Mckenzie, *Too Late for Yesterday*. And the winner is . . ."

As I began to open the envelope, I felt something drip on my nose. I knew I was sweaty, but this was ridiculous. I quickly brushed off my nose. Weird. My fingers were red. I glanced at them quizzically and then it registered. Blood! I looked up. Something was hanging in the rafters far above the stage. Slowly my mind wrapped around what I was seeing. A body.

And a dead one at that.

Just as the horror set in, the body disengaged from whatever it was hanging from and dropped several feet. Poised in midair, still attached to a chain, it began to spin around and around . . . and then it dropped again.

Right next to me.

Right where Jackson was supposed to be. The crowd sat stunned. I tried not to but couldn't help looking at the distorted, bloated face.

It was Jackson!

Chapter 3

This wasn't at all how I had foreseen the day going that morning when I started to get ready for the Emmys.

It had been a beautiful Friday morning in Venice Beach. The beach wasn't yet crowded. Even though it was the middle of June, people hadn't quite started the mad rush. My new show, *The Bare and the Brazen*, had gone dark, meaning we didn't have to work that day. This allowed actors time to get ready for the biggest show of the year. And believe me, it took some time. I had begun the day around ten a.m. by going down Washington Boulevard, around the corner from my place, to a little nail salon. Two of the girls, Ki and Luann, gave me a mani-pedi. As I was having my feet massaged, I thought I had died and gone to heaven. This was a luxury I just didn't indulge in very often, I guess because I liked to think of myself as fairly low maintenance. Maybe I needed to rethink that! By noon I was back home, standing in my bikini in my living room, slowly going around in a circle as one of the makeup artists from the show, Bobby, sprayed me with a tan. Yeah. Cancer free, takes five minutes, instant gratification, California tan. Sort of. Bobby worked on the show as a makeup artist and also free-lanced as an airbrusher. You need a tan quickly? Call Bobby. It cost about a hundred bucks, but, hey, I could write it off. And it looked so good in photos.

Once Bobby finished with the spraying, and we finished coughing up the fumes, he took out his makeup kit and started dabbing on some foundation with a sponge. One-stop shopping. Tan and makeup all in one. We decided to go with smoky eyes. A little dark liner under the eye and dark shadow blended on the top, and a pale lip. Very Brigitte Bardot. Or, if not done properly, very Rocky Raccoon. I thanked Bobby and wrote him a check for four hundred dollars. He wished me luck, saying he'd be watching tonight's show. As he was leaving, George was walking up. Georgie is my best friend. He had also been my hairdresser on *The Yearning Tide*.

"Here he is, the Emmy Award–winning hair-dresser himself."

"Yeah, yeah. Now maybe you'll give me some respect."

George had just won an Emmy the week before for Hairstyling at the Creative Craft awards held at the Sheraton in Universal City.

"I am so proud of you. You certainly deserve it," I said as I hugged him. "Now, enough about you— what about me? Or rather, what about my hair?"

"It's got to be up, sweetie. It's so fucking hot out-side! Wait, I have something for you."

George had a case I thought was for curlers and spray, but instead of hair products he pulled out a little martini shaker and two glasses.

"You have got to be kidding. Martinis, at two in the afternoon?"

"What? It's the Emmys. It's basically just one big party. And besides, the show tapes early in LA and live to New York, which is three hours ahead. That means it's really five o'clock. Cocktails!"

I hesitated before saying, "Oh, what the hell. I'm not driving," and grabbed a glass. "But just a little."

I sat down and Georgie started to work his magic.

"What the hell is this thing?" He had picked up a hair dryer I had brought out. It kind of looked like Buck Rogers's ray gun.

"What? I got that from the Emmy gift room the day before yesterday."

"You've got to be kidding me. What else did you get?"

"Oh, nothing. Well, just some perfume. And two pairs of designer shoes. Oh, some underwear by Spanx. A juicer and a George Foreman Grill."

"Is that it?" he asked with a smirk.

"Actually, no. I also got a gift certificate to a Beverly Hills spa, a six-month gym membership, a vacuum cleaner and a five-day trip to Cancun."

"Unbelievable! The people who need the least get the most."

He was joking. I thought.

"Now, c'mon. Don't be bitter. You're just jealous! Besides, I think we have to pay taxes on these 'gifts' now. And I do share. In fact you can take that fancy hair dryer with you, if you're nice to me."

"It's a deal!" He grabbed it and put it in his case.

We laughed and talked about this crazy business we were in until the doorbell rang. I got up and there was my stylist, Mara, holding a humongous garment bag and a smaller bag from Van Cleef & Arpels.

"Ooh, I wanna see!" Georgie shouted as I unzipped the bag. It was a true unveiling. I slowly lowered the zipper and carefully pulled out the padded hanger, revealing a caramel-colored silk chiffon creation of fabulousity.

"Wow! That is gorgeous." I was truly blown away. "And the Jimmy Choos. Oh, my Lord." I would tell you about them, but how do you begin to describe a pair of shoes of such sublime beauty? Thankfully I didn't have many addictions anymore. I'd given up cigarettes years ago and bad boys shortly after that. But shoes? Never! The jewelry was gorgeous as well. A big gold diamond cuff for my wrist and matching diamond drop earrings. Kind of nerve-wracking wearing them. I'd have to sell the house if anything got lost.

I wrote yet another check to Mara for finding the shoes and for making arrangements for the loan of the dress and jewelry. Jeez. Getting stuff for free was expensive.

"Remember, Alexis! I'll be backstage after the show to get the jewelry. I have to return it to Beverly Hills tonight."

"You got it, Mara. Unless I try to make a run for it. Ha-ha." She wasn't laughing as she walked out the door.

"You are a vision!" George said as he led me to the mirror. "Now, put the dress on. What time is your limo coming?"

Just then I heard a knock at the door and Connie came bursting in.

"Doll! We gotta go. We're gonna be late. We don't

want to miss the red carpet. All the press is there but they close the doors of the Kodak Theatre at four thirty. The traffic. Ahhh. It's gonna be bad." My manager and date for the evening took a much needed breath before noticing I was still in a fluffy pink robe. "Oh, my God. What are you doing? Get your dress on."

George and I looked at each other and then he went over to her and firmly placed what was left of his martini in her hand.

"Get a grip, Connie. You have lots of time. Drink up."

Connie started to protest and then thought better of it and took a gulp. "Wow. That's nice." She put the glass down. "Let's go."

I went into my bedroom, carrying the dress and shoes, and quickly threw them on. As I walked backed out into the den, I tripped over the train. A sign of things to come.

"Wow, Al! Nice," Connie said. "Really gorgeous. What a gown. I see best-dressed lists in your future. We got to go!"

"You look great, sweetie. And your hair." George put his fingers to his lips and kissed them.

He turned to look at Connie and frowned.

"You, on the other hand . . ." He quickly grabbed a rat-tail comb, and within thirty seconds Connie went from looking disheveled, hot and sweaty to a mixture of a Kim Novak and Amy Winehouse look-alike with a gorgeous French twist. "Now, about the makeup—"

"I'll touch up the makeup myself."

"I'm not talking about touching it up, darling," he said. "I'm talking about toning it down."

"Nobody tones me down, sweetie," she said, "so don't even go there. Thanks for the help with the hair, but back off."

"Gladly," George said, holding up his hands. "Wouldn't want to offend Miss Congeniality."

"Aww, sweetheart," she said, smiling up at my friend, "jealous 'cause you want to wear my crown?"

"There ain't one inch of you I'm jealous of . . . *sweetheart*," George shot back, "especially those extra inches on your butt."

Connie huffed off to reapply the pound of eye shadow she always wore. I looked at George and shrugged, trying not to laugh.

"Excuse me, Ms. Peterson? I'm Mike, your driver. We really have to go. Traffic, you know?" The limo driver had poked his head in the door.

"Of course, Mike. We'll be right out. Thanks." Then I turned to George. "Thank you so much. This was fun. Watch tonight. And pray that I don't trip." I squeezed a couple hundreds into his hand. He opened his mouth to protest. "Don't even think about it!"

He kissed my cheeks and grabbed his stuff. "Thanks for the hair dryer!" he yelled as he headed down the walk.

Connie and I shuffled out toward the limo, being careful not to drag anything or scuff our shoes. I love limos. They always make you feel festive.

We got in the car. I smiled. "This is gonna be fun, huh? I'm excited. Like George said, it's just one big party!" Yeah, right. One big murder party.

Chapter 4

I don't mind admitting I was freaked out, but it was nothing compared to the chicken-without-a-head act they were doing backstage and in the control room. The director was screaming at somebody, anybody, to drop the curtain.

I was hustled off the stage and then bumped and jostled as people started running around.

"Are you all right?"

I turned. Dave Crane's assistant, Kenny, was eyeing me solicitously.

"Yes, I—I think I am," I said. I looked down at my hands, which had blood on them. They were shaking. I tried to stop it by wringing them but that just flung the drops around. Finally I started rubbing my hands together so it wasn't so noticeable. Maybe I wasn't doing so great after all. In the end I just held them out, trying to keep the blood as far away from my gown as possible.

"Why don't you go and wash up?" He seemed to have a hard time looking me in the eye.

"Yeah, I will in a minute." I stared back at the center of the stage.

Somebody had succeeded in lowering the curtain, but now people were just standing around, staring at poor Jackson's body, trying to avoid stepping in any blood. At least they were smart enough not to try to lower him all the way.

Special security had been hired for the awards, and they took charge, locking the place down, not allowing anyone to leave. The police arrived quickly, flooding the auditorium with uniforms. People were getting antsy. The self-important were demanding to be released. The TV cameras had been turned off; the station must have put on some other programming.

Connie had come backstage to stay with me. I think it was more for her own sake than for mine, though.

"I don't know how you can stand that," she said when she saw me.

"What?" I asked.

"You look like something out of one of your early horror movies. You have blood on your forehead," she said, pointing, "and in your hair. Uh-oh. It looks like that borrowed bracelet got it, too."

I looked down at my wrist, and sure enough, the cuff had drops of blood on it.

"I'm sure that's the last thing the jewelry store thought would happen," Connie said.

"Have you seen Mara?" I asked. "I have to get this stuff back to her ASAP." My eyes were darting all over. While looking around for Mara, I realized this place was a logistical nightmare!

"I hope the cops are blocking off the rear exits. There are a lot of ways someone could get out of here." I looked up at the ceiling of the auditorium. "Not to mention, I'm sure there are trapdoors up there leading to the roof."

Connie stared at me.

"What?"

"Who the hell are you, anyway? What is it about murder that brings out your Nancy fucking Drew?"

I didn't tell her that I was trying not to scream, which had been my first instinct when I saw Jackson's body. My whole body felt tense as I continued to force that scream back down my throat.

Uniformed police started to gather near Jackson's body.

Connie had a tight hold on my arm.

"Connie, you're cutting off my circulation," I told her, freeing my arm from her clutches.

"Oh, sorry," she said. "I'm not as hard-boiled as you. All this blood is making me queasy."

I took offense to that. "I'm not hard-boiled, Connie. I feel awful about what's happened to Jackson. I can't even comprehend it. . . ."

"Yeah . . . whatever. This is some fuckin' tragedy, very sad." She paused. "But it could work for you."

Connie, ever the opportunist. Now who was hard-boiled? I know how she works, but this was just a little over the top.

"I don't want to cash in on Jackson's death."

"Why not? Look what your involvement in Marcy's death did for you."

"Yeah, I had to leave a job I loved."

"You did a movie after that, didn't you?"

"It went straight to DVD. Connie, I can't talk about this now."

People rushed past us, off the stage, on the stage, most of them with panic-filled, glassy eyes. They didn't know where to go or what to do.

"Uh-oh," Connie said.

"What?"

"Boyfriend cop at eleven o'clock."

I went to three other places on the dial before I finally found him. Detective Frank Jakes.

"He's not my boyfriend."

"Here he comes," she said. "I'll . . . go find Mara."

I turned and saw Jakes walking toward me, followed by his partner, Detective Len Davis. Since they hauled Marcy Blanchard's murderer out of the canal behind my house months ago, Jakes had called a couple of times to try to set something up. The first time he said he needed to tie up a few loose ends. I put him off and tied up his faux loose ends on the phone. The second time he asked if we could have a drink. I begged off. The third time he actually asked me out to dinner. I told him I'd call him back. I never did. That had been a month ago, and he hadn't called since then. God, I thought now, that had been so mean. . . .

The problem—well, not actually a problem, per se—was I had a boyfriend, Paul Silas, a crime scene investigator in private practice. The other problem was I had found Jakes attractive at the time, and watching him walk toward me now, it was clear that hadn't gone away. If anything, he looked even better.

I'd forgotten how blue his eyes were.

"You didn't have to get yourself involved in another murder just to see me," he said as he reached me.

I looked past him and said, "Hello, Detective Davis."

"Ms. Peterson. Frank, I'm gonna . . ."

"Okay."

Davis faded away.

"Alex?"

"Yes? Oh, I'm sorry. What did you ask me?"

"I asked how you were," Jakes said, "but maybe I should ask how you are?"

"I'm not so good, Detective," I said. "Jackson was a friend of mine. I've got his blood on me." I held my hands out to him like a frightened little girl.

"You knew the deceased?" He was looking at me funny when he asked this. My dress left little to the imagination but he didn't have to be so obvious.

"His name is—I mean was—Jackson Masters," I said. "We're on the same show, and we were supposed to present an award together. He was running late, or a no-show, we all thought, but then . . . this." I waved at the stage.

"Uh-huh," he said, staring at me.

I looked him square in the eye and raised my eyebrow. "Do you think this is really the right time and place, Detective Jakes?"

He looked at me, puzzled, and then it registered. He smiled. "Alex, go wash up. . . . You're a mess."

"I can't."

"Yes, you can. Come back because I have a few questions for you. Don't worry. I don't think you're going to make a run for it!"

"No, I mean I can't. You're on my train!"

He stepped aside, revealing two dark and dirty footprints clearly imprinted on my extremely expensive borrowed gown.

We looked at each other.

"Stupid train," I grumbled as I made my way to the bathroom.

Chapter 5

When I got into the ladies' room and saw myself in the mirror, I nearly lost it. Connie hadn't told me exactly how awful I looked. There was blood in my hair, on my forehead, and on the bridge of my nose. No wonder Jakes had been looking at me like that. I even had blood in my cleavage. Before I tried to fix myself, I ran into one of the stalls and suffered some dry heaves. I was lucky I hadn't eaten much before coming to the theater.

I did my best with paper towels and lukewarm water, and then I tried to get my hair back into some semblance of order. When I finished up I looked like a member of the B-52s. Only not as good.

I left the ladies' room and worked my way backstage. Everything was still in chaos there as well as in the front of the house, where the cops were taking names and addresses.

Connie spotted me and started over.

"Al, I found Mara. They won't let her come over here before they finish questioning people. I'll give her the jewelry." She held her hand out. I took the earrings and cuff off and gave them to her.

"Thanks, Connie." She walked off to the back of the stage. I turned and saw Jakes coming toward me.

"Hey, you look . . . better."

"Thank you." I tried to muster up a little dignity. "So, what happens now?"

"This is a crime scene. We're locked down."

"Are you going to let people go home?"

"Eventually," he said. "As soon as we get all their particulars."

"You could get a complete list of attendees from the producer."

"That'll be helpful," he admitted, "but there's bound to be some people who aren't on the list. Seat fillers. Event crashers. Right?"

"Yeah, a lot of seat fillers."

"Okay, so we're gonna be here a while."

"Do you know how poor Jackson was killed?"

"They're taking him down now," Jakes said. "I didn't see any obvious wounds. He's bleeding, but we can't tell from where. The chain is around his neck. We'll need the ME to answer your question."

"Oh."

"Do you have to get home to your daughter?" he asked.

"No." I hesitated before I said, "Uh . . . she and my mom are out of town."

"Really? I thought you and Sarah were glued at the hip."

"Oh, yeah. We are. It's just that it's a family reunion back east. I couldn't get off work so I sent them without me." I was nodding my head up and down as I said this. Why did this guy make me so nervous?

"Okay . . . so do you want to leave?" he asked. "I

can have somebody take you home. How did you get here?"

"Limo," I said. "I can go home the same way."

"Well, if your driver's in the building, he won't be getting out until late."

"I see."

He wasn't looking at me when he asked me the next question. "Do you want to call your boyfriend to come over?"

"No." I hesitated just a hair too long. "He's out of town . . . on location."

Then he looked at me. And held my eyes. "So I can have someone drive you home," he said, "or . . . you can wait around and I'll drive you myself."

"Aren't you keeping me here as a suspect? Like last time?"

He smiled. "No, this time I'm not looking at you as a suspect."

"Why not?"

"I don't think you would have been crawling around up in the rafters in that dress."

"Thanks for that."

"So, that ride?" he said.

"Okay."

"Okay, what?"

"I'll wait around for that ride . . . with you," I told him. I had a lot of questions to ask about the case. I couldn't help myself and tried to convince myself my interest in true crime was the only reason I wanted to ride with him.

"All right, Alex," he said, lightly touching my arm. It was unnerving and weirdly thrilling all at the same time. "Is there any coffee around here?"

"Sure," I said. "There's craft services back here, for the show's hosts and presenters. Come with me."

Gradually people began to leave the auditorium. But behind the scenes, nobody was going anywhere because they had all been close to the body when it fell. Apparently everybody backstage qualified higher on the list of potential suspects than people in front of the house did. If Jakes was telling the truth, I was the exception.

But based on all of my past dealings with Detective Frank Jakes, I knew he couldn't be counted on to always tell the truth.

But then again, who could?

Chapter 6

"Okay," Jakes said when we were both in his car and heading for my house, "fill me in on this Jackson character."

"Jackson Masters is—was—one of the young hunks of the soap world."

"What does that mean exactly?"

"A lot of the time," I said, "it means not much acting talent but great abs."

"A lot of the time?"

"Jackson had some talent. I think in a few years he would have developed his acting chops and had a decent career."

"So who didn't want him to move on?"

"You got me."

"No ideas?"

"None."

"Come on, Alex," he said. "You're my in to the soap world—my expert."

"Sorry, Detective," I said, "but on the set Jackson was pretty well liked."

"And off the set?"

"I didn't socialize with him."

"Did he ever come on to you?" Jakes asked.

"What a cliché! Not all actors come on to each other! We're not always jumping in the sack with anything that moves!"

Jakes was quiet.

I was quiet, too. The fact of the matter was that soon after I joined *B&B*, Jackson did hit on me. Or, at least, he flirted. I hated having to tell Jakes he was right, but I also didn't want to get in the way of his investigation. If Jackson had been killed *because* of the way he hit on women, then I needed to come clean.

"Okay, so shut up. He hit on me once," I said, "but I brushed it aside, didn't pay much attention to it, and he moved on."

"To other women on the show?"

"I suppose," I said. "I'm the newest actress on the set, so he had probably already gone through the others."

"Gone through?" he asked. "You mean, slept with?"

"No," I said. "Yes . . . I don't know. I mean, maybe he'd slept with some of them. . . ."

"Do you know which ones?"

"I'll have to think about it. If I tell you," I asked, "will they be suspects?"

"Maybe," he said, "or maybe their boyfriends or husbands."

Damn. I hadn't wanted anyone pointing a finger at me last year when Marcy was killed, so I hated to be the one to point at anyone now.

"Let me think about it," I said again.

"You do that," he said. "Take all night. Get back to me tomorrow."

"I'll try."

He pulled up in front of my house and turned off the car. "Dark house," he said.

"I told you, my mother is away and has Sarah with her."

"Yeah, I remember you said that." He turned in his seat to look at me. "Why didn't you ever call me back, Alex?" he asked.

"C'mon, you know why. . . . I have a boyfriend." I felt like a teenager in high school.

"How's that working for you?"

I was tongue-tied.

"Get back to me tomorrow with some names," he said, turning to face the windshield again. "Nobody will know they came from you. I just need a place to start, and I'd appreciate your help."

"All right," I said. "I'll see what I can do."

"Good night, Alex," he said. "Nice seeing you again."

I didn't quite know what to say—"Nice to see you, too," sounded lame—so I just got out of the car, pulling my dirty train out with me, and watched him drive away before I headed for a shower.

Chapter 7

I opened the door and carefully locked it behind me. I was immediately hit with a blast of silence. My mom had taken Sarah back to the Midwest to get to know her cousins and aunts and uncles at an extended Peterson family reunion. She would be there for at least two weeks. This part was all true. But there was another, more important reason behind the trip.

A few weeks ago I had received a phone call from my son-of-a-bitch ex-husband, Randy. The guy who had taken money set aside for my early retirement so I could be a stay-at-home mom. He had fled the country and I had not heard from him in three years. He hadn't always loved me, but he had always loved our daughter. And now here he was calling to say he was coming back to the States in a couple of weeks to see Sarah. I knew Sarah missed him, even though he had left when she was so young. She still remembered him and had recently started asking a lot of questions about her daddy. I want her to have a father. I'm just not so sure her biological dad is the best candidate for the job.

Anyway, I told him I needed to think about things

and to call me back in a couple of days. Would he go to prison? I wondered. I guess that would depend on what his other clients did. I wasn't the only one he took money from. In any case, it would probably be minimum security for a few months, maybe a year, since it was a white-collar crime. Would he want shared custody? I didn't think I could stand that. So I promptly changed my number. I needed a few days to think and I had this invitation to the family reunion. Knowing I couldn't make it, I bought a couple of plane tickets for my mom and Sarah—just in case Randy tried contacting her. I never mentioned it to anyone, not even my mother. The two of them being gone for a while gave me a chance to think.

I looked around and saw Flipsy Dog and his brother, Flipsy Doggy—Sarah's toys we had gotten from an outdoor vendor at the Third Street Promenade in Santa Monica. I picked up Flipsy Dog and smelled him, hoping to get a little Sarah. No luck. Flipsy needed a bath. He smelled like stale peanut butter. I held onto him tightly and went to the phone to check my voice mail. Hopefully my ex hadn't gotten my new number. Thank God only Paul had called. He was on location with the TV show he was serving as consultant for, and he had seen the awards on TV.

"I just wanted to make sure you're okay, honey," he said. "I'll try to call again tonight, but we're doing a night shoot and there's no signal out there."

I wasn't sure where "out there" was. All I knew was that he was in Canada, somewhere near Vancouver, and would be for several more weeks.

"I'll try to call again when I get back to the hotel," he said. "Meanwhile, call me there and leave a message. I need to know you're okay."

I really didn't feel like talking to Paul at that moment. I wasn't sure I could keep the guilt out of my voice—even though I had nothing to feel guilty about. Not technically, anyway. All I'd done was talk to Jakes. Okay, so it was a little more than talking, but not really. A little flirting, maybe. Not even. But I felt sure Paul would hear something in my voice.

I chanced it and was relieved when I had to leave a message on voice mail. I simply told him I was okay and would talk to him soon.

I called my mom next, hoping Sarah would be sleeping because of the time change. I knew Mom would be worried. Naturally, she'd watched the show.

"Alex," my mother said, "don't get involved again."

"Mom, I have no desire to get involved. Only if it's pretend and I get paid a lot of money for it."

"I don't believe you."

"Mom, is Sarah okay? Did she see the show?"

"Thank heaven she fell asleep before it started. That would have been too traumatic!"

"You're right, thank heaven for that." I felt lonely. And sad. And a little scared. "I really miss you guys. Give her a big kiss for me and make sure she gets lots of veggies tomorrow, okay? Tell her if she doesn't eat her fruits and veggies, she won't poop and her tummy will hurt. That always does the trick. I'll call back in the morning. . . . I love you."

"I love you, too," she said. "Alex . . . stay out of trouble."

I peeled off my gown and jumped into a nice hot shower. I watched the water pool and then spiral down the drain. Blood followed. Jackson's blood. I shivered and found myself welling up. I let the hot water wash my tears away. For the first time since I'd seen his dead body, I let myself feel for him. He was just a kid.

I blearily grabbed for the phone, knocking it off its cradle. It was only five a.m.

"Mommy, I saw a possum. . . . He looked like a giant rat."

There were a lot of possums in the Midwest, along with squirrels, raccoons, deer and many other animals my daughter had never seen except in a petting zoo. She was all excited and talked until she ran out of breath. Then I told her I loved her and missed her, and I must have air kissed the phone ten thousand times before she said she had to go because there was a squirrel outside the window.

I hung up, made coffee and barely had time to sip it when the phone rang again. It was Paul.

"Are you okay? What the hell happened last night?" he asked.

"No one knows anything yet. I mean, Jackson was obviously murdered, but that's it so far." I didn't know what else to say, so I said, "How are you? How's the shoot going?"

"Worried about you, Alex. Since when did acting become such a dangerous occupation? Are you really okay?"

"I'm a little shaken up for sure. But I'll be all right."

"I think I need to come home and see for myself."

"No!" I said a little too quickly. "I'm fine, really!"

He took a long pause, and I heard him sigh impatiently. "Don't you need me, Alex? Just a little bit? Still with the independent bullshit! Trying to do it all on your own, huh?" He sounded annoyed and . . . hurt. "Have it your way. If you decide you want some support, let me know." And he hung up.

What was wrong with me? Why couldn't I let this great guy in just a little? I threw my coffee into the sink.

"Fuck it! I need to get wet." I decided to do a little surfing. When your whole life is falling apart, what else is there to do? Besides, it would give me a chance to think about what Jakes had asked me to do . . . and Randy . . . and *not* Paul . . . and Jakes. . . . Too damn many men.

I grabbed my nine-foot-six board and threw it in my SUV—which I call my kid car, since I drive Sarah around in it—along with a towel and some wax, and I backed out of my garage.

Immediately I heard, "Alex! Alex! Over here!"

"What happened last night? Did you have anything to do with this murder?"

No way. Not the paparazzi. Again. I looked around and saw one old guy with a camera. I guess I wasn't such a major player in this story. Thank God.

I yelled out my window, "I have no comment. I know nothing!"

And then I felt kind of sorry for him.

"If I find anything I can share with you, I'll let you know!" Lame. Lame.

I rolled up my window and drove down the street to a soft beach break, making sure the old guy wasn't following me. I started walking toward the ocean. The sand squeezed through my toes. I love that feeling. It's cool and moist, and I feel peaceful and excited all at the same time.

I paddled out into the waves and found a good

spot. Surfing is my meditation. It gives me a chance to really think without distractions.

I sat on my board and looked toward the sand. The sun felt wonderful. I was actually starting to relax when I noticed a man pacing back and forth on the beach. He would stop now and again and then look out toward the water and . . . me. At first I thought it was paparazzo, but he looked like someone I knew. Someone I had once been married to, actually. Was that Randy? He wasn't supposed to be back for weeks.

After a few minutes he turned around and walked away.

Randy was creepy but not that creepy. I decided I was just being paranoid and started thinking about the gossip that goes around the set of any show. Like who was sleeping with whom, because that stuff is hard to keep quiet. I could easily have given Jakes the names of half a dozen women Jackson had slept with, or who I thought he had, anyway. And that wasn't just from our show. The question was, did I want to? No, maybe that wasn't the question at all. He was a policeman running an investigation—but on top of that he was someone I had come to trust and admire, even if I had been avoiding him for six or eight months. If I gave him the names, I knew he wouldn't go off half cocked, threatening people or locking them up.

A nice, juicy wave appeared on the horizon. I waited for it to take shape and slowly began to paddle in front of it. As soon as I felt it behind and beneath me, I gave one last strong paddle and I was up. I rode it all the way in. One was going to have to do today. I walked over to my towel and picked up my cell phone. Jakes answered after the first ring.

"How about lunch?" I said.

"I thought you'd never ask."

We met halfway between downtown and Santa Monica at a little café off of Robertson. Not the trendy part by The Ivy and Kitson. A little south of there, where the paparazzi didn't gather.

"If you don't mind," I said, when we were seated, "I have to justify this to myself."

"Justify away."

"If I give you some names, I need your word—"

"I promise it'll never get back to them," he said, cutting me off. "I won't say a word about my source."

"No, that's not it," I said. "I don't want the names getting into the papers. I don't want these people's lives ruined because of my big mouth."

"I promise," he said. "I won't even tell Len where I got them."

"Don't be silly," I said. "He's your partner."

"Maybe not much longer."

"Why not?"

"I'm up for promotion," he said. "If I get it, we won't be partners anymore."

"Really?" I asked. "Where does that leave him?"

"Promotion? No, not Len."

"Why?"

"Let's just say he's not the promotion type," Jakes said. "Len's gonna be right where he is now until he retires."

"And what about you?" I asked. "Where are you going to be?"

"Probably in another squad."

"Oh? Where?"

"In another part of the city," he said. "Don't worry, Alex. You're not gonna get rid of me that easily."

"I'm not worried— I didn't mean—"

"Anyway," he said, "I guarantee that nothing will happen with those people unless, of course, I find out one of them is the killer."

"Well," I said, "they're all women. I don't think any of them would be strong enough to pull Jackson up into the rafters."

"A woman could have had an accomplice," he said. "Besides, the body wasn't secured very well up there, which is why it fell when it did."

"It wasn't supposed to fall then?"

"Apparently not."

"How was he killed?"

"He was stabbed," Jakes said. "Then he was tied sort of haphazardly with the chain—"

"Why a chain?" I asked. "Why not a rope?"

"We don't know," Jakes said. "Maybe there was no rope available. Anyway, the body slipped, the chain got wrapped around the neck and . . . well, you know the rest."

"Only too well."

We paused as the waitress came with our food. Jakes had ordered cottage cheese and a salad. I just looked at it.

"What? Actresses aren't the only ones watching their weight. Cops like to avoid heart attacks, too."

Then we looked at my greasy fish and chips.

"I guess I'm in need of comfort food. Let's just move on."

"Okay, Alex," he said, taking out a notebook. "I'm ready."

"I can't prove any of this, okay? I mean, I wasn't

there. And personally I have a hard time believing anything unless I see it with my own eyes. There is so much BS in the rags, and people make up—"

"Alex, I get it, okay? When you think you maybe, sort of, have an idea, could I possibly know?" he interjected.

"Well, word has it on the set that Jackson and this actress on the show may have had something. Their love scenes were just a little too real. And you could see he was slipping her the tongue. Which means he was probably personally invested. And that's just not done."

"What do you mean not done?"

"With professionals, there is no exchange of bodily fluids. In other words, you fake it. You move your lips and head in such a way that it looks real, but it's not!" I found myself going through the motions of a stage kiss.

I stopped when I realized he was staring at my mouth. Flustered, I dug into my bag. I pulled out a *Soap Opera Digest* I'd picked up at the market earlier. Shayne Weaver was on the cover.

"This is her. Shayne Weaver. She's pretty, huh? Doesn't look like a murderer. And by the way, she's small . . . only five-four."

"Save me all the reasons why she couldn't be the killer. Who's next?"

"There's Penny Mason. Makeup artist who works only as a sub. She comes and goes. Bev Cartwright: she's a stage manager. I heard that maybe a little somethin' somethin' could have happened when he first started out as an under five on another show. Th—"

"Wait. Under five?" Jakes asked.

"Oh, yeah, you don't know. An under five is a performer who has under five lines. Not quite a full role . . . not quite an extra. You got to start somewhere, right? As I was saying, I also heard about Jackson and Mandy Tessler. She's another actress on my show. They dated a while and she broke it off. I don't know why. And everyone heard about his thing with Marty Humphries. She works in the office as a casting assistant. Some say she helped him get the job. Probably just gossip. But then again, isn't everything?" I thought I'd covered everything.

"Christ! How long had this guy been on the show? When did he sleep? Are you sure that's it?"

"No. But it's all I know about. And remember, it could all be bullshit. But I doubt it. But don't hold me to it, okay?" I wasn't thrilled about giving over the information. But maybe, if it would help find Jackson's killer, I could live with myself.

Chapter 8

He wrote all the names down, pausing only to pop one of my fries into his mouth. I noticed I was going through my lunch a lot faster than he was and tried to slow down.

"So these are the women you think might have hated Jackson enough to kill him?"

"No," I said slowly, "these are the women I happen to know could have possibly slept with Jackson."

"Do you know how they each felt when he ended the relationship?"

"Detective—"

"Aw, come on, Alex," he said. "You gotta start callin' me Frank."

"Would you mind if I call you Jakes? You just don't seem like a Frank to me," I said. "Okay . . . Jakes, from what I know and what I've heard, Jackson wasn't really into relationships."

"Do you know that for a fact?"

"Know what?"

"That this superstud didn't have a girlfriend."

"Well . . . no, I don't know it. I suppose he could

have had someone on a more steady basis, but if he did I never met her."

"Which would make her a pretty good suspect," he added, "if she found out about these other women." He finished his water. "Coffee?"

"Sure, why not?" I wanted to ask some more questions of my own.

Over crème brûlée and coffee—my crème brûlée; his coffee—I asked, "Who's claiming the body?"

"Why do you want to know?"

"Just curious."

"Well, no one so far," he said. "We haven't been able to locate any family. We went through his apartment and found an address book."

"A little black book?"

"Actually, it was green," he said. "We've got somebody calling all the numbers, trying to identify the people attached to them."

"Isn't that a little cold?" I asked. "There's bound to be a relative in there, and your somebody is just going to blurt it out that Jackson's dead."

"Well, number one, no," he said. "We're just trying to find out who's who. Nobody's going to be told anything about him being dead."

"And number two?"

"Number two, somebody in that book is bound to have been watching TV yesterday."

"So they'd already know."

"And maybe they knew he was dead before the show," Jakes said. "We'll get around to questioning the likely suspects in person. Hey, maybe we'll even find a girlfriend in there."

"You'll probably find a lot of girls in there."

"Is your name among them, Alex?"

"What's that mean?"

"I was just wondering if you ever played a scene with Jackson."

"A love scene, you mean?" I asked. "On or off the screen?"

"Hey, Alex, I'm just askin'—"

"Okay," I said, "when I first joined the show, we had a scene together. Our characters were supposed to have a history, so in flashback they showed us . . ."

"Showed you what?"

"We had to do a bed scene."

"A bed scene? And this is your *job*? Was there any tongue?"

"Of course there wasn't any ton— Oh, shut up."

He smirked.

"So," I went on, hating to have to say it, "you're right that he hit on me once, and you're right that we had a scene together . . . once."

"Was that so hard?" he asked.

"Yes," I said, "yes, it was."

"In what way was it *hard*, exactly?" He could barely contain himself, the bastard. I just looked at his smug but handsome face.

We finished our dessert, he paid the bill and we went outside. I'd tried to chip in, but he would have none of it.

"Off to work?" he asked.

"No," I said, "we don't work on Saturdays."

"So what will happen now?" he asked. "Will the Emmys be rescheduled?"

"I don't know," I said. "That's up to the network—

and I guess they'll consult with the producers from all the shows. They could just hold a press conference and announce the winners."

"Seems to me if they broadcast the show another night, they'd get big ratings, with everybody tuning in to see if another body fell from the roof."

"Sadly, you're probably right," I said.

"Will you go back?" he asked. "If they call and tell you they're gonna do that? Would you go and present the award you were supposed to present with Jackson?"

I paused before answering. Would I? And if I did, would I be able to resist looking up above me for another body?

"To tell you the truth, Jakes," I said, "I really don't know."

We were walking toward our cars. He had been there when I pulled in and had waited for me to get out of my car so we could walk in together. Now we simply retraced our steps.

"Have you ever won?" he asked. "I mean, an Emmy. I'm sorry, I'm not up on these things. . . ."

"Yes," I said, "I've won twice."

"Best actress?"

"Yes," I said, "but that was years ago."

"Well, that doesn't matter," he said. "I mean, how long ago it was. It's still quite an accomplishment."

My cell rang out, "Young man"—you know, "Y.M.C.A." from the Village People. Jakes rolled his eyes and said, "When are you going to change that?"

"I know, I know." I looked at the caller ID. "I need to take this. It's my manager. One second. Hey, Connie, what's up?"

"Here we go again, doll! *Star* and *OK!* both want to talk to you about the murder last night! How ironic it is that you have now been involved in two murders—last year, and now this."

"Connie, I have no comment and I really don't want to deal with anything else right now. I have way too much on my plate." I felt my blood pressure rising. I knew what was coming.

"I know, I know, Al. It's been tough." She had no idea. "But I see big things in your future. We gotta strike while the iron is hot. Remember what happened after the Marcy thing? Work happened!"

I couldn't take it anymore. Not this again.

"I don't want any more work, Connie! I am perfectly happy where I am. Am I making myself clear?" I guess I was screaming because Jakes looked at me with concern on his face. "Look, Connie, I'm sorry. I just really think we need to take a break. Too much is happening."

"Sure, Al. I'll call you in a couple days when—"

"No, let me call you. Okay? Let me call you. It's not personal. I love you. I'm just fried. I'll call you." And I hung up.

"Are you okay?" Jakes put his hand on my arm; I was afraid I was going to cry. I took a deep breath.

"Yeah. I'm okay." Clearly I wasn't. The murder and Paul and the whole Randy thing were wearing on me.

"Is this about your daughter?" he asked. My head jerked up. How did he know? "You miss her, right? I know how close you are."

Should I tell him? God knows I wanted to tell someone. I just didn't want to open that can of worms. Not now.

"Yeah, I miss her so much." He cocked his head to one side as if waiting for me to go on. When I didn't, he put a supportive arm around me and walked me to my car. He waited while I unlocked my door.

"Alexis," he asked, "can I call you again?" I must have looked as confused as I felt.

"I mean," he hurried along, "if I have any more questions about soap operas and the people who work in them. After all, this is only my second TV-related murder."

"Well," I said, starting to open my door, "in that case I can't very well refuse, can I?"

"No," he said, "you can't. Do me another favor, will you?"

"What's that?" I asked, pausing with my door half open.

"Keep your ears open when you go back to work."

"And what am I listening for, exactly?"

"Anything," he said. "Anything at all about Jackson Masters. Maybe somebody has some info, an opinion, about him that might be helpful."

"You know, there are some people who are going to be glad he's dead," I said. "That doesn't necessarily mean they killed him."

"I know that," he said. "I'm just asking you to . . . be alert."

"Okay, I can do that."

"Thank you."

He came close to me and put his hand on my arm. For a moment I thought he was going to kiss me. I caught my breath, but then he stepped away so I could fully open my car door.

"Take care of yourself, Alex. If you need to talk—about whatever—give me a call."

Getting in my car, I nodded and then started the engine. As I pulled away I tried not to look in the rearview mirror but couldn't help myself. There he stood, watching me drive away.

Chapter 9

Instead of going home, I drove to see my best friend. When he opened the door and looked at me, he said, "You look awful, darling. Who's doing your hair these days?"

"Not an Emmy Award–winning hairdresser, that's for sure," I said.

"Come on in," he said. "We were just about to have some 'tea.' "

His partner is a writer who worked from home and rarely left during the day. He only seemed to come out of the house when the sun went down.

"Rustle up another batch of martinis, Wayne," George said as we entered their kitchen.

"It's kind of early for drinks," I said.

George gave me a deadpan look and yelled out, "Make them weak. We've got a stick-in-the-mud here!"

Wayne rushed over and gave me a hug.

"You poor thing," he said. "I saw it on TV. It must have been awful for you."

"It wasn't that good," I said. "When I realized

blood was dripping all over me, I didn't know what was going on."

"Do they know who killed him?" Wayne asked.

"How was he killed?"

The questions were coming fast and furious.

"Take it easy," I said. "Give me a 'weak' martini and I'll tell you what I know."

I waited until we were all seated with martini glasses close by before I told them what I knew. Most of it came from Jakes—but I didn't tell them that.

Wayne was too sharp for me, though. "Did you learn all of this from your hunky detective friend?"

"What hunky detective friend?" I asked, making my eyes as innocent as I could.

"Alexis," George said.

"Oh, you mean . . . Jakes?" I'm a pretty decent actress . . . most of the time.

Wayne laughed. "Look, she blushes when she says his name."

"I'm not—" I started, my hands rushing to my face. Then I realized I'd been had.

"You're mean," I told them.

"He's mean," Wayne said, pointing at his partner. "I'm nice."

"Okay, okay," I said, "so I got the information from Detective Jakes. So what?"

"So nothing," Wayne said. "I was just asking."

"Never mind him," George said. "So, what's on your mind, Alex? Are you going to play detective again?"

"No, of course not. I mean, I don't think so," I said. "I just— It was just a shock, you know? To have that happen? And I knew Jackson. I think if there's something I can do . . . to help find out who did it . . . I should do it, right?" Hoping to distract them, I handed George my cell phone. "By the way. Could you help me get rid of my ringtone?"

"Why do you want to do that?" George asked innocently.

"Why do I want to do that? Because ever since you put 'Y.M.C.A.' from the Village People on my phone I've been a laughingstock. Seriously, it was fun . . . for a while. But let's try something new. And not the Village People."

"What would you like? You can pretty much have anything you want."

I gave him the evil eye. "Just nothing too embarrassing, okay? I am a mother and an established TV star." I playfully punched him on the arm.

"Ow! That hurt, sweetie!"

"Oh, shut up. You are such a wuss!"

"Oh, and Detective Jakes is a strong, hunky hero, right? Did he ask you to get involved? Because he needs your 'help'?" George was not one to be distracted. "Or because he wants to flex those muscles for you?"

"Whatever the reason, I say do it," Wayne said.

"I have a boyfriend."

"You're not in a committed relationship, are you?" he asked. "An exclusive, committed relationship?"

Well, we didn't see other people. I knew Paul wanted it that way. At least he did before our last conversation. But now I wasn't sure I did. Even before meeting Jakes when Marcy was killed, I had my doubts that Paul was right for me.

I'd first found Jakes very annoying, and then attractive. Paul had sensed it and become jealous. By the time Marcy's killer was caught, I knew Jakes was interested, and the last time we'd seen each other he'd kissed me.

After that I had studiously avoided him and begun paying much more attention to Paul—out of guilt, I guess. Not really the perfect platform on which to build a relationship.

Now Jakes was back, and I was glad, very glad. Was that why I'd agreed to help him? Well, it wasn't the only reason. I did want whoever had killed Jackson to be found. So where was the harm in helping Jakes? It wasn't like I'd begged him to let me help. He had come to me, right?

Paul would never understand, though, and I knew it.

"I'm not sure where Paul and I are exactly," I said, finally answering Wayne's question. "We're committed to each other, I guess. He's a great guy! I care about him so much. I just don't know why I can't let him in more." I looked at my friends and almost cried. "What's wrong with me?"

"Nothing's wrong with you, sweetie. Maybe it's not meant to be. There's only one way to find out, though. Help Detective Jakes and maybe you'll see what that's all about. Once and for all," George said. They both looked at me, the troubled single friend, with the kind of compassion only a happily committed couple could.

"After all. You have nothing to fear but fear itself." Wayne added.

"Didn't FDR say that during the Great Depression?" I looked at them, grimaced and then grabbed my glass.

"I'm trying to save you from your own personal depression," Wayne said, pouring me a little more pink fabulousness. "You could be missing out on something wonderful because of fear."

"You're right. I've been afraid to find out how I really feel because then I'll have to do something about it. I'm going to help Jakes and figure things out."

"Cheers!" George said.

"You go, girl!" Wayne added.

We all raised our martinis and toasted. I'm sure I appeared more confident than I really was.

Chapter 10

When I went back to work on Monday, it was obvious Jackson's murder had affected everyone. There was a deep sense of mourning. Jackson was well liked, and you could tell people were in a state of shock. Everyone was quite solicitous toward me . . . wanting to know if I was doing all right and how I felt when Jackson's body came tumbling down at me on stage.

Sammy Horner, known as Timber because his huge belly made him "equilibrium challenged," was directing that day. I'd worked with him on *The Yearning Tide*. He moved around from show to show, covering for other directors on vacation or whatever.

"Okay, okay," he yelled, "grill Alex on your own time, kids. She needs to get to hair and makeup. I know it's a sad thing but we have to get moving. We've got a show to do. Jackson would want us to."

What an idiot. Jackson would want us to? Jackson would want us to take the day off and go to the beach. That's what Jackson would want. But I was a professional and agreed that the show must go on. So I went to my dressing room to drop off my stuff and pick up my script. Then I headed off to hair and makeup.

"Awful, just awful," Mary, my makeup artist, said. "It was too awful! I mean, poor Jackson! And you, standing up there. It was like something out of a Greek tragedy. You in your gown. You looked beautiful, by the way. Then the blood dripping down your face. I mean, it was tragic. Truly like something out of an old Bette Davis movie. Or a Stephen King novel . . ."

"I get it, Mary. I was there, remember?" This was getting a little hard to take. I had to work today, after all, and stay focused. Thank God I was just playing one character today: Felicia. "Could you please just finish my lips?"

I looked at her in the mirror, saw a tear roll down her cheek. She was a pretty girl in her early twenties, and at that moment I wondered if she had just been another notch on Jackson's belt.

"I'm sorry, Mary. I didn't mean to be so harsh. This is just all getting to me." I pulled back to really look at her. "How well did you know him?" I asked.

"Not well," she said. "Oh, I mean, he was nice enough to me, even flirted a little, but . . . that was all. We just . . . talked while I worked on him."

I wasn't sure if I believed her or not. I guess it was possible she just had a lot of unrequited feelings for Jackson Masters.

"Do you know anything about his family, Mary?" I asked.

"Not really. I mean, I got the feeling he wasn't too close to his family, you know? It's just so sad. So, so sad. And tragic. What a tragedy . . ."

I jumped out of her chair. I couldn't take it anymore. "I'll finish up my face myself. Thanks."

She was still sniffling when I left her.

* * *

My hairdresser's name was Henri. The only thing he had in common with George was that he was gay. In fact, Henri had a very unpleasant personality, which I discovered during my first week on the show. He was good at what he did, though, so we'd developed a safe way of working together.

We hardly spoke, except to talk about my hair.

That was why I was surprised when, as soon as my fanny hit the chair, he asked, "Do you know how Jackson was killed?"

I looked at his reflection in the mirror. He was younger than George, in his early thirties, and quite good looking.

"Sorry?"

"Jackson Masters," he said. "You were there. Do you know how he was killed?"

"From what I understand," I said, "he was stabbed."

His face was blank, but his shoulders slumped.

"Henri—"

"How do you want your hair today?" he asked.

We talked about it for a few minutes and came to a decision, and he went to work.

"Henri, how well did *you* know Jackson?"

"We . . . talked," he said.

I found that odd. As far as I knew, Henri talked to hardly any members of the cast.

"Did he ever talk about his family, or maybe a girl-friend or something?" I asked.

"It doesn't matter now, does it?"

"It might."

He dropped his hands from my hair and stepped back. Our eyes met in the mirror.

"Come on, Henri," I said. "What do you know?"

"You're some kind of . . . amateur detective, right?" he asked. "At least, that's what I've heard."

"No," I said, "I was— No, I'm not any kind of detective."

"But last year, there was a murder and you were involved."

"I was involved in the murder *investigation*. That's true." I could tell he was itching to say something but I needed to tread lightly. "You can talk to me, Henri. I mean, if you need to."

He looked around. For the moment we were alone, but that could change in an instant. "All right. I do need to talk to someone . . . but not here."

"Why not?" I asked. "There's no one—"

"Not here," he said. "We should meet later, at the end of the day."

Obviously he had too much to say to risk being interrupted or overheard. I just hoped it would be something useful.

"Okay," I said. "Where?"

It surprised me when he asked if I would come to his apartment that evening, and he wrote down the address for me. It was in West Hollywood. I agreed.

After he finished my hair, I got out of the chair to go to wardrobe, and he called out to me. "Hey."

"Yes?" I turned to face him.

"Don't tell anybody, all right?" he said. "No cops?"

"No cops," I said. "Promise."

Chapter 11

My scenes that day were pretty good actually, considering everything that was going on. Felicia was in the midst of trying to figure out who had stolen her identity and was wreaking havoc with her credit cards and such. Of course, it would be revealed later that it was her evil twin, Fanny, who was trying to discredit her. My scenes were with Jerry Thomas, who played my husband, Dmitri. Nice enough guy. A little full of himself but that was nothing new. We worked well together, and the day went quickly. But not quickly enough for me. No matter how much I fought it, I found myself excited about going to see Henri. I had hoped that the whole Marcy murder had taken the amateur detective right out of me, but Nancy Drew was alive and kicking . . . hard. What I should have done was call Jakes and tell him that Henri apparently knew something, and then let Jakes go and get it out of Henri. But I hadn't. How could I? After all, I had made Henri two promises. One, that I would go to his apartment, and two, that I would not call the cops.

So I drove out of the studio lot and headed over to

West Hollywood to have my conversation with Henri, a man who—until today—I had exchanged barely ten words with that didn't have something to do with hair.

What, I wondered on the way, could Henri have possibly had in common with Jackson Masters? They certainly hadn't exchanged conquest stories, had they? Everybody knew Henri was gay. But he didn't look gay. In fact, if you had stood Henri and Jackson side by side and asked people to pick out which one was gay . . . Wait a minute.

The thought struck me, and I shook my head. Was it possible that Jackson was gay? And that he and Henri were lovers? Jackson had a big rep as a womanizer. But he could have been bi. Stranger things have happened. Maybe he just liked sex and didn't much care who he was with when the urge struck.

Henri had an apartment in an old Spanish style stucco fourplex in West Hollywood. It was probably built in the twenties and was very well maintained. There was a time in the 1970s when West Hollywood resembled Hollywood and became rundown. The buildings were dilapidated, and drugs and prostitution were on the rise. But no more. West Hollywood had become home to a large gay community and was clean, safe and beautiful because of it.

I climbed the concrete steps and looked at the four doorbells. Next to one was the name Henri Marceau. I rang the bell, but there was no answer. I rang again. At that point a man rushed out the door and down the steps without looking back. I barely registered his green T-shirt and jeans before I caught the door and went inside. The tag next to the doorbell said Henri was in 2B. I went up to the second floor and found 2B. The door was ajar.

I knocked. "Henri?"

No answer. Had he forgotten I was coming?

The smart thing for me to do would have been not to go inside but to pull out my cell phone and dial 911. I never said I was smart.

I could feel that old familiar feeling. Adrenaline. Here I was, déjà vu all over again.

"Henri," I called. This time I pushed the door open and stepped inside. The apartment was a mess. Somebody had been fighting or maybe looking for something. I listened but couldn't hear anyone moving around. It looked to me like a three-room apartment. I was in the living room, and I could see a small kitchen. There was one other doorway, possibly to a bedroom. There were also French doors opening to a small balcony. No one was out there. I walked to it and found it locked.

Okay, I thought, the bathroom.

I moved to the other doorway and looked inside. The bed was made, dresser drawers were hanging out, no laundry in sight. I moved inside and crossed to a closed door I felt sure led to the bathroom.

"Hello? Henri?" I knocked on the bathroom door. No answer. "Henri?"

That was when I started to become concerned. I had three choices: Get out, call 911 or open the bathroom door.

I opened the door.

Of course.

When Jakes walked in, he stopped to talk to the two cops before coming over to me. I was sitting on

Henri Marceau's sofa. He was dead in the bathtub, where I had found him about an hour before.

"Let's go out on the balcony," Jakes said.

"Okay."

He slid the door open for me, stepped out after me and closed it. The balcony overlooked the front of the building.

"What the hell, Alex?"

"What? You asked me to help."

"Don't play stupid. What are you doing here?"

"Henri does—did—my hair on the show."

"So you came to his apartment for . . . what? A haircut?"

I gave him a look.

"Okay," he said, "why don't you just tell me what you were doing here."

"Henri wanted to talk to me," I said, "only he said he couldn't talk at the studio. He wanted to talk in private, so he asked me to come here."

"Talk to you about what?"

"Jackson Masters."

His eyebrows went up. "He knew somethin' about Jackson Masters?"

"I suppose so."

"And he wanted to tell you?"

"He wanted to tell somebody."

"Did you think to recommend the police?"

"He didn't want to talk to the police."

"He might have a record," he said. "I'll check on it. So you came here and . . . what? How'd you get in?"

"His door was ajar."

"No, I mean how'd you get into the building?"

"Oh, uh, well, I rang the bell, and while I was waiting for him to answer, another man came running out. I realized after the fact that he could be the killer. . . ."

"Or he could be just another tenant. I'll find out who they are."

I grabbed his arm and then realized what I was doing and released it like it was hot.

"How was he killed?"

"I don't know," he said. "I haven't been in there yet. Look, stay here and wait for me. I just want to go inside and get the lay of the land."

I looked down at the street, filled now with vehicles with flashing lights. I could see my car, blocked in by the others.

"I've got nowhere else to go."

"Okay, then. I'll be a few minutes."

He slid the door open and then stopped and looked at me.

"What?" I asked.

"You know," he said, "you find more bodies than any civilian I know."

"I didn't find Jackson," I reminded him. "He fell on me . . . almost."

"Yeah," he said. "Yeah, you're right about that. Okay, I'll be right back."

"I'll be right here," I assured him as he went back inside.

I meant it when I said it, but then I got bored so I walked down to the yard, toward the bushes and pathway the guy who had run by me had used. Who knows? Maybe he had dropped something. I was just trying to make myself useful.

Chapter 12

I didn't find anything except dog poop and an old piece of chewing gum, so I went back to the balcony and watched the action through the sliding glass door. Men in blue, men in white, men in suits came and went. Every so often Jakes would look over at me and signal with his finger that he'd be done soon or would join me soon, or maybe he was telling me that I was number one.

I finally got tired of watching the comings and goings of the LAPD and turned to study the buildings across the street. People were at their windows, watching the action. They were probably wondering what the hell was going on. Lucky me, I was in the know. I had found the body.

I wasn't that experienced at finding bodies. Marcy last year, her husband a few days later, and now Henri. Jackson didn't count. I didn't find him; he sort of found me.

Suddenly I started to sob, and tears came into my eyes. I felt so overwhelmed. Another murder was bad enough, but I had yet to deal with Randy. I found myself looking over my shoulder for him. Maybe

I should tell Jakes. As if on cue two arms enfolded me from behind and turned me around. I cried into Jakes's chest. I still didn't understand my feelings for him but it felt pretty good.

I was settling in a little too comfortably so I jerked away. "I'm sorry. How girlie of me."

"That's okay," he said. "You are a girl, aren't you?" He said this with appreciation. I did feel so female with him and wished he was still holding me. My nose was running. He wiped it with a tissue he'd pulled from his pocket.

"You're in shock. Let's go someplace and have a drink."

"My car," I said. "It's blocked in."

"I'll drive. By the time we come back, some of those vehicles will be gone."

"Um, you want to talk to me some more about the . . . the murder?"

"Yes," he said. "Yes, I do, and I don't wanna do it here."

We didn't discuss anything until we were seated in a small café near the beach.

"I haven't had dinner; have you?" he asked.

"No."

He smiled. "Then why don't we have dinner?"

"Will I have to make a statement about today? A written statement?"

"Sure," he said. "You can do it after dinner or come to Parker in the morning. Your choice."

I scratched my head. "If I do it tomorrow, it'll have to be very early. I have to go to work."

"Early's no problem," Jakes said. "But why don't you tell me what you know now?"

"I've already told you everything."

"Tell me again," he said. "Start from the beginning, when you first spoke with Henri today. And try to do it word for word."

Chapter 13

I repeated everything I'd told him already, trying to remember Henri's exact words.

"And that's it?"

"That's all of it," I said, playing with my shrimp scampi. "We didn't say much at the studio—we never do. I mean, it's not like we're friends."

"Really? I thought women were always friends with their hairdressers."

I gave him a withering look. "That's such a cliché," I said. "He doesn't really talk to anyone."

"But he talked to Jackson Masters," Jakes said. "That's what he wanted to tell you."

"Yes."

"But he never got the chance."

It was a statement, not a question.

"Okay," he said, "so you get to his building and . . . what?"

"I rang the bell, there was no answer, but like I told you, the other man came out and I caught the door."

"Okay, we'll deal with this other guy later," Jakes said. "What happened when you got upstairs?"

"The door was ajar. I knocked, called out, but got no answer. That's when I started to worry."

"So that's when you should've called 911."

"And told them what? That a man didn't answer his door? No, I had to go in. I mean, he could've been hurt and needed help." We both knew I was tap dancing. When I saw the mess the apartment was in, I could have called 911.

"Tell me what you saw."

"A messy apartment. When I got to the bathroom, I found him there in the bathtub, just . . . lying there."

"And then you called 911?"

No, I thought.

"Yes," I said.

I didn't tell him that my innate curiosity and fascination with all things dead got the better of me. I admit it: it's a character flaw. But it's *my* character flaw. And besides . . . I might have found a pulse.

"Alex, did you touch anything?"

"Of course not! What do you take me for? Don't answer that!"

"Not even a doorknob?"

I just looked at him. "No."

"Okay."

"How was he killed?"

"His neck was broken," Jakes said. "Somebody wrapped something around his neck and snapped it."

"Ewww. What do you think they used?"

"That we can't tell," Jakes said. "Whoever did it took the weapon with them."

"So he wasn't stabbed like Jackson."

"Actually," Jakes said, "they were killed the same way."

"How do you figure that?"

"Turns out the stab wounds didn't kill Jackson Masters."

"What did?"

"The fall from the catwalk," he said, "and the chain around his neck."

"You mean . . ."

"He was hanged," Jakes said. "That chain snapped his neck at the time of the fall. He might have died from the stab wounds eventually, but he didn't have the chance."

"Oh, my God."

"I feel pretty certain that the same person killed them both," he said. "Was Jackson gay?"

"Not that I know of, but . . ."

"But what?"

"I was thinking the same thing."

"Maybe that's what Henri wanted to tell you?"

"Yes."

"We found Jackson Masters's number in an address book in Henri's apartment. That, in itself, doesn't mean anything."

"But?"

"I found this also in the address book."

He took out a strip of photos, the kind you get from one of those machines in arcades and malls. There were four shots of Jackson and Henri together, smiling, laughing, and—in the last one—Henri was kissing Jackson on the cheek.

"Jackson doesn't look happy in this last photo," I said, handing it back.

Jakes had been plowing through a bowl of whole-wheat pasta while we talked. He put the photos back in his pocket and continued to eat.

"Well, it could be that Jackson was either gay or

he went both ways," Jakes said. "That would increase our suspect pool."

"Maybe . . ."

"Maybe what?"

"Maybe it was a one-time thing," I said. "I mean, with Henri."

"You mean that Henri was just so adorable, Jackson couldn't resist?"

"Not my words," I said, "but essentially, yes."

Jakes sat back and scratched his head, pushing his plate away as if something was ruining his appetite. I'd never seen any evidence of it before, but I suddenly wondered if he was homophobic.

"I don't buy it."

"Why not?"

"I think people are straight, gay or bi," Jakes said. "I don't hold it against any of them. But I don't think anybody switches sides just once."

"What if it was his first time with a man?" I asked. "And he didn't like it, so he never repeated the experience."

"That's possible, but I think Jackson was just too sexually experienced to have tried it with a man only now, at this age. I think it was more likely he tried it in his teens and liked it, but not exclusively. The picture I've been getting of Jackson Masters is that he pretty much knew what he liked. He seemed to be some kind of . . . pleasure hound."

I don't know why it should have surprised me to realize he'd been talking to others about Jackson, but after only a moment I realized it made perfect sense. After all, he couldn't depend just on what he'd learned from me.

"So you've talked to the women he's slept with?"

"Some of them," he said. "One or two are still denying it—due to husbands, boyfriends—but whatever the reasons, I'm sure they'll come around."

Our waitress came over and Jakes asked me, "Coffee?"

"Please."

"Any dessert?" she asked Jakes, pointedly ignoring me.

We ordered our desserts and she went off.

"Are you surprised?" he said.

"About what?"

"Jackson being bi or gay?"

"Believe me," I said, "those photos in your pocket are a shock to me."

"Because it was a man, or because it was Henri?"

"Either way."

"Well," he said, "I'll have someone go through Jackson's address book with a new eye."

"How's your partner, by the way?" I asked. "Still . . . mad at me?"

"I think he's more hurt than mad," he said. "He thinks you've . . . Tiffany's abandoned him."

Len Davis had been a big soap fan when I met him—and an even bigger Tiffany fan, the character I had played on *The Yearning Tide*.

"You know, I was never sure if that was an act or not with him."

"Oh, it's no act. He's a real soap junkie—particularly *The Yearning Tide*—and especially when it comes to you—or Tiffany."

My coffee arrived, and the rest of the meal went by too quickly. "I have a question," I said, when we were in the car, driving back to Henri's place.

"What is it?"

"If Jackson's been sleeping with men as well as women, he's been keeping it quiet," I said. "Why would he allow those pictures to be taken?"

"You know," he said, "that's a very good question— and with both of them dead, we'll probably never get an answer."

He pulled up in front of the building. All but one of the official cars were gone. The one left might have been the original car that responded to my call.

Before I got out and switched to my car, I asked, "What about the man I saw running out of the building? Was he a tenant?"

"Could be," Jakes said. "We got a description of tenants from the building manager, and the guy could be a match. I'll have to check it out." He put his hand on my arm as I reached for the door. "Before you get out of the car, Alex, I have a question for you."

"Okay."

"Why the hell did you go into that apartment?" he asked. "Didn't you think about the danger?"

"Only at the very end," I said, "when I found the door open. But when I was ringing the bell and getting no answer, it never occurred to me that anything was wrong. I just thought he wasn't hearing me."

"Even when that other man came running out of the building?"

"Like I said," I answered, "I thought he was a tenant."

"And like I said, he might be," Jakes said. "I'll find out, but I still wish you hadn't gone into the apartment when you did. You could have gotten hurt. Where's your damn boyfriend, anyway? Isn't he supposed to be watching out for you?"

"First of all, he's out of town," I said, bristling, "and second, no, he's not supposed to be looking out for me. I generally look out for myself."

"Okay," he said, backing off. "I didn't mean— Hell, after what happened last year—and the other night—I just wish you'd be a little more cautious."

I stared at him for a moment and then relented and said, "I guess that's good advice." I felt my eyes welling up again. Oh, shit! I didn't want to go all girlie on him again. So I looked down at my hands and played with my ring finger. I looked up and Jakes was staring at me.

"What?" I said defensively.

"Isn't there something else you want to tell me?"

"I don't know what you're talking about. I'm just . . . tired. And I miss Sarah. That's all." I tried to look blasé.

"Really?" he asked, looking surprised. "That's it? I kinda thought you'd fight me a bit more."

"I don't want to fight anybody, Jakes," I said. I was so close to telling him about my ex. I just couldn't. Sighing, I added, "I do want to help, though."

"Okay, then the next time you find somebody you think has some info, call me, will you?"

"I will," I said. "I promise."

I meant it at the time. . . . I really did.

Chapter 14

I went into my house, poured myself a merlot (Oprah's Dr. Oz says it's good for me and I love him for that) and then carried it out back to the yard. I stood there sipping and staring out at the canal.

After the police pulled a murderer's body out of the water last year, I thought about moving. The main reason I didn't was Sarah. This was her home, she was comfortable here, she had her room and I didn't want to take any of that away from her. She had gone through so much in her short life. Basically losing her dad and a life as she knew it. So we stayed. And after a while it had gotten so I hardly ever thought about almost being killed behind my own house. I thought I had put those incidents completely behind me, but now they were back. Thanks to Jackson Masters being murdered; thanks to Detective Frank Jakes thinking I could be helpful. I was so close to telling him about Randy. What was stopping me? I could be so stubborn. Always thinking I had to handle all of life's shit on my own. I had to be the strong one. Like Paul always said. Well, so far in my life, I *did* have to be the strong one.

Did I need to examine my motives? Sure, I enjoyed flirting with Jakes—or having him flirt with me—but I had also lost a friend. Okay, not a *close* friend, but a friend who had almost fallen on me, who had certainly bled on me. Well, it was a tragedy. And like it or not, I was involved. I guess I was just trying to justify my involvement.

The truth was I found being involved in another murder—and with Frank Jakes—exhilarating. And that was something I was not going to be able to admit to anyone else. How heartless that would make me seem.

I was deeply lost in thought when "Let's Talk About Sex" came blasting from my cell. Funny, George! I was going to kill him! I answered it and was brought up short by a familiar voice.

"So you changed your home phone but not your cell? That is so unlike you, Al. You're usually so much smarter than that." It was Randy. And he sounded pissed.

"Look, I just wanted some time to think without you bugging me every five minutes, okay? Obviously I knew you could get a hold of me if you really wanted to." I thought about adding "asshole" but didn't.

"So, how's my little girl?" He still had a sexy, kind of raspy voice. It used to make my knees, and brain, weak. It didn't have that effect on me anymore.

"All of the sudden you care, Randy? Where the hell have you been the last three years when she cried for you, wondering where her 'Daddy Bear' was? You have some fucking nerve. Taking money I worked my ass off to make and breaking my little girl's heart." I had waited a long time to take off on this bastard and it felt good.

He paused and I could hear him deciding what to say. He answered me in a measured tone.

"She's my little girl, too. What I did was fucked up and I'll do my best to make it up to you both—"

"You son of a bitch! You can't make it up to either one of us!"

"Listen, Alexis! No matter what I've done, you can't keep me away from Sarah. I'm warning you, don't even try! You think your life was tough after I left? You have no fucking idea how tough I could make it for you!" His voice was shaking. How could he muster that much indignation? "I want to see Sarah. . . . Don't fuck with me!"

"Fuck you!" I said, and hung up. I hadn't even asked him if he was in town. I was rattled despite wanting to remain calm, cool and collected. If he had been trying to scare me, he had succeeded. And that pissed me off, too. Just then my cell rang again. I almost threw it across the room until I saw it was Jakes.

"Just calling to check and see that you're okay."

"I'm fine, Jakes," I said. "I'm fine."

"You don't sound fine. What's going on?"

"Nothing, just tired . . ."

"Look, I know something's been eating at you for quite a while . . . besides murder. I'm trying to give you your space, but I can tell from the tone of your voice something is going on and it's not good!"

I was quiet and then I relented. "You're right. Something is going on but I don't want to get into right now. Maybe another time?"

"Yeah, of course. But are you okay for the night?"

"Yeah, definitely. I'll see you tomorrow. Bright and early on my way to work."

"Good," he said. "Bring coffee. The stuff we make here is awful."

He hung up before I could ask him how he liked his.

I was ready for bed later when I picked up the phone and dialed on a whim.

"Hello?"

"George, it's Alex."

"Alex, sweetie," he said. "Are you all right?"

"Yeah, I'm good." I was, in fact, not good at all, but I needed to hear a friendly voice. "I just wanted to thank you for that snappy ring tone. Very funny. And tasteful."

"I thought it was appropriate for you under the circumstances." He laughed. "By the way, how's that going for you?"

"I don't know, George," I said. "I think I might be in trouble."

"What kind of trouble, hon?"

I told him about my afternoon with Detective Frank Jakes.

"And?" he said when I finished.

"What do you mean, and?"

"Well, did he kiss you?"

"No, he didn't kiss me."

"Honey, how can you be in trouble if he didn't kiss you?" he asked. "It sounds like the two of you spent the afternoon around a dead body, talking about other dead bodies. When are you going to get to the good stuff?"

"I don't want to rush anything!"

"Rush anything? This has been simmering for over a year! Would you just kiss him already?"

"Maybe I should wait for him to kiss me . . . ?"

"He kissed you first last year! It's your turn! Or whatever! Someone kiss someone already! Call me back when you're really in trouble!"

"All right! I get it. Good night!" I hung up and just lay there for a minute. Had I always been so inept with men? Yes, I believe so. I snapped off the light and hugged my pillow.

When I was shown into the squad room the next morning, Jakes was sitting in his shirtsleeves at his desk, a grim look on his face.

"Don't tell me," I said, putting the bag down on his desk and fishing out a container. "You thought I'd forget the coffee."

He leaned forward, snagged it and pried the lid off.

"Good," he said. "Black, the way I like it."

I took the second container out for me and sat down opposite him. "So, why the long face?"

"New developments."

"Like what?"

He touched the computer on the stand next to his desk and said, "Stupid fucking machine. We put the MOs of these two killings in here, and what do you think popped out?"

I felt oddly privileged to be on the inside, sitting in Parker Center, across from Jakes, being let in on new developments in the case. I looked around but didn't see Jakes's partner anywhere. I did see several other men watching us, though.

"Don't mind them," Jakes said, as if reading my

mind. "They've never seen a real live diva this close up before. They're jealous."

"Diva? Why diva? I'm an *actress*, for Christ's sake. Just when I was starting to like you!" I had a thing about being called a diva . . . obviously.

"Sorry. Jeez. Actress. They've never seen a real live actress!" He leaned forward. "Anyway, the computer kicked out four other cases where the MO is similar. Now I've got to follow up and see just how similar they really are."

"Sounds like a lot of work."

"Lots of footwork," he said. "That's why I get the big bucks, though."

"What about the women?" I asked. "The names I gave you? And Shayne Weaver?"

"The Weaver girl is alibied," Jakes said. "Of the women whose names you gave me, two slept with him, but there was apparently no relationship. They didn't know the others."

"Can I make my statement?" I asked. "As it is, I'm going to be late to the set."

"I thought we were going to talk about what's bothering you, Alex." He looked at me pointedly.

"No, that's okay. It's really nothing I can't handle. I just came to give you my statement, like you asked."

"Okay, sure. But you will tell me later?" he asked, and I nodded. "I'll have someone take down your statement and type it up, and then you can sign it."

I sipped my coffee and said, "That's fine."

"Just wait there," he said, sliding his chair back. "I'll be right back." He paused and turned to me. "So, you're starting to like me, huh?"

I sort of smiled.

He walked away, taking his coffee with him. On his desk was a piece of paper with four names written on it. I leaned over, trying to read them upside down.

"Damn," I said.

Chapter 15

"Wait a minute," Jakes said moments later when he returned with a civilian woman who was going to take my statement. "You're telling me you know these guys who were killed the same way as Masters and Marceau?"

"Not all four," I said. "I recognize one name." I pressed my finger to the paper, still lying flat on his desk. "That one."

We were both standing on his side of the desk, so that I was seeing the list right side up for the first time.

"Aaron Summers?" he said.

"He is—was—an actor who auditioned for a role on my old show, *The Yearning Tide*."

"When was this?"

"Last year."

"Did he get the role?"

"No."

"Okay," Jakes said, "so he was an actor. Jackson Masters was an actor. What about these other two?"

"I don't know them."

"So how do I find out if they were also actors?" he asked.

"Call AFTRA or the Screen Actors Guild," I said. "If they were actors, they would have been members. Unless they weren't union yet. But that's a good place to start."

"Okay," he said. "Okay, good. Thank you. Barbara will take your statement now, and as soon as you sign it, you can go to work."

"Thanks."

"No, Alexis," he said. "Thank you." He grabbed his jacket from the back of his chair, looked at Barbara and said, "Use my desk."

"Yes, sir," she said.

He started away and then turned and called out to her, "Have you seen my partner?"

"In the break room, watching TV."

He looked at me, shrugged and left.

"Thank you for joining us, Alex!" the director, Richard Breck, called out.

"I know: I'm late," I said apologetically. "I'll get right to wardrobe." I didn't offer an excuse. I didn't want to draw attention to myself. Frankly, I was tired of that kind of attention. I had had enough of it last year on *The Tide*.

Breck was tall and lean, the exact opposite of Sammy "Timber" Horner. Timber was usually brought in when a show needed to be taped fast, often for budget reasons. Breck was a whole different animal, a man who took his time and made sure he got the scene to his satisfaction.

"We've moved your scenes, Alex," he said. "Had to move on without you, you know."

"I know, Dick," I said, waving. "Don't worry. I'll be ready."

When I got to the back, talk in wardrobe, hair and makeup was all the same—the murder of Henri Marceau. It was obvious that Henri hadn't had that many friends. People were definitely shocked and upset by his murder, but I wouldn't say anyone was actually sad. The discussion went on as they worked on me to get me ready for my scenes. Apparently no one knew I had been there at the murder scene, because it never came up, which suited me.

They did, however, ask me my opinion.

"First Jackson and now Henri. It's such a tragedy! One right after the other!" Mary said when I was in her makeup chair. "What do you think is goin' on, Alex? Is our show jinxed?"

I didn't want any part of this discussion. I just buried my head in my script and shrugged.

"Or maybe it's just soap operas in general. Look what happened on your old show last year, right?"

I was watching her face in the mirror as it hit her.

"Hey, that's right," she said. "Somebody was killed on that show, and now this one. Maybe it isn't the show that's jinx—" She stopped herself by slapping one hand over her mouth. "Oh, Alex, I'm so sorry. The way that sounded—"

"Never mind, Mary," I said, brushing it off. "Let's just get me finished, huh? The director's already pissed off because I was late."

She started sniffling. I looked up, and sure enough, she was crying. I mumbled something comforting and bolted for the door.

* * *

We shot my scenes for the day, and even with perfectionist Breck at the helm, we got through them quickly.

"I hate to say this," Breck said when we finished the last scene, "but maybe you should be late more often, Alex. You were great."

"Thank you, but I wasn't in those scenes alone." Actually, I was. Both of my characters were talking to each other on the phone. Very heated and emotional scenes as Fanny had begun to blackmail Felicia with information only she knew.

He came close to me and said, "Very funny, darling. It was all about you today—but seriously, do me a real big favor."

"What?"

"Try to be on time tomorrow."

"I promise I'll do my best. And don't call me darling." Maybe my racquet was strung just a little too tight, but it took every fiber of my being not to smack him across his smug face. I hate smugness.

Chapter 16

I went to my dressing room to clean up and get back into my street clothes. By the time I was dressed I had an idea. I made a phone call, and when the call was answered, I said, "Can you meet me tonight?"

"Of course—but you still want to talk to me, after what happened last year?"

"I'd like a favor," I said. "Let's just say you owe me."

"Okay," he said. "Where?"

When I knocked on the door, Andy McIntyre opened it himself. Apparently he had not felt the need to replace Murray the Life Coach.

"Hey, Alex," he said. Impulsively he grabbed me and hugged, and I hugged back. I realized at that moment that since leaving *The Yearning Tide*, I'd missed him and that show. "Come in."

I followed him to the kitchen, where he had already put on a pot of coffee.

Andy and I had started on *The Yearning Tide* at the same time. In fact, we had played young lovers at one point.

"We can drink it out by the pool," he said.

"That's fine."

He armed us both with a mug and we carried it outside. The house was in Malibu, not far from Paradise Cove. He had an impressive view of the beach.

"I'm so happy to see you, Alex," he said as we sat. Then he started in with questions. "How do you like your new show? The new characters? Are you having fun playing dual roles? I smell Emmy!"

"Yeah. I mean, it's harder but it's a blast," I said.

We talked a little about the new show, and then he filled me in on what was going on with *The Tide* and all its characters. It felt a little like the old days, when Andy and I used to talk a lot. I have to admit, I also felt a little left out.

"*The Tide* is not the same without you."

"That's nice of you to say, Andy."

"It's true," he said. "We miss Tiffany."

"When I was there, everybody thought I was a murderer," I reminded him.

"And, for a shorter time, they thought the same of me," he said.

"So how can you continue to work with people who thought you were capable of that?"

He smiled wanly and said, "I'm not a beautiful soap star who is in demand, Alex. I'm an aging soap actor who's happy just to have a role."

I had said Andy and I started on *The Tide* at the same time and that we'd been cast as young lovers, but truthfully, he was a good eight or ten years older than I was. He had lost his glow and he was no longer a heartthrob.

But today was the first time I realized that he was a

sad, middle-aged man. But he was still my friend, so it made me sad, as well.

"So, what can I do for you, Alex?" he asked.

I got myself back to the reason I was there. "As I said, I need a favor. Have you ever heard of an young actor named Aaron Summers?"

"No," he said. "Is he another of those baby hunks all the shows are hiring?"

Spoken like a former young hunk, I thought.

"I remember he auditioned for a role on *The Tide* a while back," I said without answering his question.

"Really, Alex," he said. "Why are you trying to track down young actors—"

"Not young actors," I said. "Just this one."

"What's so special about this one?" he asked. "You think he's right for something on your show?"

"Hardly," I said. "He's dead."

"Oh, jeez, the Emmys," he said, slapping his forehead. "I meant to call you. I'm so sorry—"

"Forget it."

"But, wait—he's not the one who came down from . . ."

"No, that was Jackson Masters."

"Right, right," he said, snapping his fingers. "I read that. He worked on your show, right?"

I was surprised it had taken him so long to mention something that was the talk of our industry. Then I was surprised it had taken me so long to realize that he'd probably been drinking before I got there. If he'd worked that day, he could only have been drinking an hour or so before I showed up. I looked at my coffee. I'd already had a few sips, and it wasn't spiked. I'd watched him pour it, so his wasn't spiked, either.

If Andy still drank the way he used to, he'd probably had three, maybe four drinks.

He'd been tense when I first arrived. Now he was starting to loosen up.

"That's right, Andy."

"So are you in charge of finding a replacement? Oh, no, wait, stupid me. You already said the other man was dead."

"That's right."

He sipped his coffee, drumming his fingers on the side of the mug. I figured he was ready to have another drink, probably wanted me out of there quick.

"I need to find out the details of when Aaron Summers auditioned for *The Tide*, Andy," I said. "Can you do that for me?"

"I can ask when I get to work tomorrow! Oops, I don't work tomorrow. Or the next day, or the one after that!" His bitterness at having a lesser role in the show was showing.

"Somebody in casting will have the information. Maybe you could call?" I thought it was better if someone from the show asked about Summers instead of me. I didn't want anyone's antennae to rise.

"Okay," he said, "so I'll ask. What can it hurt?"

"Can you call me tomorrow?"

"Sure," he said, "sure. We murder suspects have to stick together, right?"

"No, Andy." I put my mug down on the table. "We old friends have to stick together."

"Can I get you anything else?" he asked. "I was gonna have dinner—"

"No, thanks," I said, standing up. "I have dinner plans."

"Oh, of course," he said, also standing. "Sarah. How is she?"

"She's fine." No harm in letting him think I had to go home to make dinner for her.

He walked me to the door, where he said, "I really was gonna call you, Alex."

"I know you were, Andy," I said. I hugged him tightly. My good friend. I felt so sorry for him I wanted to cry. I kissed his cheek. "I'll talk to you tomorrow."

Chapter 17

I was on time the next day, as I had promised. We taped my scenes with no problems, and the day ended with no further compliments from Breck.

When I arrived at my car in the parking lot, I was surprised to find Jakes's partner, Detective Len Davis, waiting for me.

"Detective. How's your son doing anyway? Davey, right?"

"He's fine. Thanks for asking, Ms. Peterson."

"You were calling me Alex last year, Detective."

"That was last year."

"I'm sorry you feel betrayed by Tiffany—by me," I said, wondering if I was going to need help from security—and, if I did, if they could get to me in time.

But Davis did not have the look of a crazed fan. I'd seen them enough times before to know. It was usually in the eyes. Or possibly their sweaty palms. Or their tendency to space invade. You know, get a little too close for comfort. Or their willingness to buy your character a present for her wedding. Or when you find out they've just been released from prison and they know every signpost on your way from work to your home. Or they threaten to kill you and security has to walk you to your car after work. I digress.

"This isn't about that," he said.

"What's it about?"

"Frank Jakes."

"What about him?"

"He's going out on a limb for you," Davis said. "Putting his career on the line."

"I—I don't know what you mean."

"By bringing you into his investigation, letting you know certain things, he's breaking the rules."

"Why's he doing that?"

"You don't know?"

I shrugged. "He thinks I can help him?"

"You're smarter than that."

"Look," I said, "I haven't encouraged him—"

"Haven't you?"

"No, I haven't," I said pointedly. "I hadn't seen him at all until . . . until all this."

"But now you've seen him a few times," he said. "Since the other day, at the Emmy show."

"Have you talked to him about this?"

He hesitated and then said, "No, I haven't mentioned it to him."

"A man was killed, Detective," I said. "A friend of mine. All I'm doing is trying to help."

"But you're not helping," Davis said. "I suggest you stay out of it and leave it to the experts."

I was suddenly pissed at being warned off. "So why doesn't Jakes tell me that?"

"He won't," Davis said. "He should, but he won't."

"Then maybe you should be having this talk with him," I said, "not me. Please move so I can get in my car."

I watched him in my rearview mirror as he watched me until we were out of each other's sight.

I was mad, but I didn't know who I was maddest at—Davis for warning me off, Jakes for putting me in this situation, or myself.

As I was driving home, my Bluetooth rang in my car. Living in Los Angeles means only hands-free cell phone usage in vehicles. I pushed the phone symbol on my steering wheel. "Hello."

"Alex? It's Andy. I got that information you wanted—"

"Hold on, Andy."

I pulled over and parked, and then took a pad and pen from the glove compartment.

"Andy, how are you?"

"I'm fine, sweetie," he said. "Fine. Yesterday I was a little . . . well, you know."

"Yeah, I know," I said. "What did you find out for me?"

"You were right. Aaron Summers did audition for a part on the show early last year. Needless to say, he didn't get it."

"Do you have an address for him?"

"Yep, here it is."

I wrote it down. Like a lot of young actors, Aaron Summers had chosen to live in the heart of Hollywood, a place called Beachwood Canyon, near the Hollywood Hills. There were lots of beautiful houses there . . . and lots of not so beautiful dives. But it is an artsy community with lots of color and history.

"Any other information?"

"Well, yeah, I got a copy of his resume and head shot."

"Can you fax me the resume?"

"Sure. Not the head shot?"

"Sure, the head shot, too."

I gave him my fax number. "Thanks for this, Andy."

"Sure, Alex, but why—"

"I can't hear you, Andy. I'm in a canyon. . . . You're breaking up!" Cheap ploy, but effective. He was about to ask me why I wanted the information or what I was going to do with it, and I didn't have an answer for either one.

I started the car and, instead of going home, headed for Hollywood.

Chapter 18

Without really knowing why or what I was going to do when I got there, I drove to Hollywood and found the house that went with the address Andy had given me. I switched off the engine and sat in my car for a few moments. I was still mad, but now I knew I was angry with Detective Davis. I was in amateur detective mode and he was spoiling my buzz, forcing me to examine not only my own motives for getting involved, but Jakes's motive for accepting—or even requesting—my involvement.

Other than the police, who had more of a right to be involved than I did, considering what I'd gone through on stage? But who was I kidding? I was hardly Carrie, standing on stage with a bucket of pig's blood pouring over me, stigmatized by the experience. Sure, having Jackson's blood smeared on my face and in my hair had been shocking, but I'd been involved in a police investigation before—even found dead bodies. I was anything but catatonic over it. Instead, it had piqued my interest, making me want to know who hated Jackson Masters enough to kill him. And then I'd walked in on poor Henri's body in his bathtub. Of course Jakes wanted to pick my brain, since I had been so close—physically speaking—to the victims, and I was deeply involved with the soap opera world, where these men came from.

Hell, I thought, defiantly opening my car door and stepping out, maybe that would sound kind of harsh to some people, but it made perfect sense to me.

The drive to Aaron Summers's address was almost a waste of time—until the end.

His landlady answered the door when I knocked, and she rocked back a couple of steps when she saw me. She put one carefully manicured hand to her intricately painted face. She was probably in her forties or fifties, trying hard to be in her twenties or thirties, and doing a pretty smashing job of it.

"Omigod," she said. "It's you!"

"I'm sorry?" But I had an idea what she was going to say.

"I watch your show every day," she said. "I mean, I used to watch *The Yearning Tide* every day. I still watch it, but now I watch your new show, too. I just love you, Tiffany—I mean, Felicia. And that Fanny! I love her accent and the way you say 'Bad, bad, bad!' What I don't get is how someone as beautiful as you are can look as unattractive as that Fanny! Hours in the ugly chair, right?"

I wish I could say that was true. But it actually took me less time to get ugly than it did to get pretty.

"Well, thanks," I said. "I'm always glad to meet a fan."

"What are ya doin' here?" she asked.

"I was looking for someone who knew Aaron Summers."

Her exceedingly large boobs heaved under her floral blouse. "Oh, Aaron," she said, sadly shaking her head. "That poor kid. He thought he was gonna be a huge soap star, ya know?"

"I know," I said. "He auditioned for a role on *The Tide* last year."

"That's right!" she said brightly. "He was real excited about that."

"Did he live here a long time?"

"No, just a couple of months." Her hand flew to her mouth. "Christ, I'm a crappy hostess. Come on in. Would you like some coffee or tea? I have some donuts but I'm sure you never eat that crap, right? Always watching your figure. I know; I read *People*." She held the door open for me.

I would have liked nothing more than to bury my head in a big box of Krispy Kremes but I didn't want to ruin the illusion.

"No, thanks," I said. "I just have a few more questions."

"Sure thing," she said. "God, my girlfriends are not gonna believe you were here."

"Did he have a lot of company during the time he lived here?"

"By company, do you mean girls?" She grinned. "Yeah, he had lots of girls—but I'm sure you know all about that. I mean, you actors."

I bit my tongue. I needed information. And besides, she had a point.

"Did you ever meet any of his family?"

"Nope, he never had family come over. Just his . . . friends."

"Men?"

"Yeah, his friends, buddies. Ball games, parties, stuff like that."

"Do you know any of his friends?"

"How do you mean know? A little flirtation here. A little flirtation there. Some of them were cuuute! I sure as hell ain't dead yet. If you know what I mean. We older girls need to get it while we still can, right?" She elbowed me in my side.

I wanted to weep. Was I truly that old? Never mind. I still needed information.

If Jakes had been there with me, he'd have known what questions to ask. I didn't like admitting it, but I had a weak bedside manner when it came to interrogation. Maybe I could take a class at The Learning Annex. "How to Interrogate Witnesses," taught by Lieutenant Columbo, or maybe Lieutenant Kojak . . . Was I dating myself? Maybe I *was* old. . . . I was flailing.

Then she perked up. "I know he had family, though. I mean, a mother and father, at least."

"Oh? How do you know that?"

"They called me, after he died," she said. "Wanted to know if he had anything of value in his place. When I told them it was just clothes and stuff, they told me to give it to Goodwill or something. That father—what a cold fish he sounded like. I still got the address written down somewhere."

"Why do you have the address if you didn't ship them his things?"

" 'Cause I told that father of his that Aaron owed me two months' rent. He bitched, but he sent me a check. You want I should try to find it?"

"Yes," I said quickly, "yes, I would. Thanks so much."

"Let me look in my closet. I just about throw everything in there. I won't be a second. Have a seat. Get comfortable. By the way, did I tell you I read tarot cards? Maybe we could read yours? Whaddya think?" She turned and walked down the hall.

Chapter 19

I heard her rustling around in a closet down the hall and then a loud yelp. "Son of a bitch! That hurt!" She turned the corner, re-poofing her flattened hairdo, and started to hand me a piece of paper. "Damn, I need one of them organizers in here. That closet is a mess, but I found it!" I reached for the paper but she pulled her hand away.

"Oh, c'mon, now! You can't go! We're just gettin' acquainted! I want to hear all about you and especially that hunky Alec Brandon!" Alec is an actor on my show who has an impressive female following. Apparently, she was one of them.

"I've had a crush on him for thirty years! I'd love to read his cards! Now, why don't I get you some coffee—or somethin' stronger, right? And you relax and we'll do a little reading." She grabbed her deck of cards and started to shuffle them.

Oh, God, it was going to be a long night if I didn't get out of there fast. I made an excuse about having to learn my lines, grabbed the piece of paper and headed for the door. "Thanks again for your help."

As I drove away I could hear her yelling, "If you

ever want your cards read, you come on over. Don't even call first!" I nodded enthusiastically and waved. And hauled out of there.

I jumped onto the Santa Monica Freeway heading toward Venice and promptly got stuck in five o'clock traffic. I pushed the phone symbol and yelled out, "Mom's cell." Nothing happened. I had been having problems with my Bluetooth voice recognition. Sometimes it took a few times.

"Dammit!" I began screaming, *"Mom's cell!"*

Finally I heard ringing and then "Hewwo?" Sarah still had a little bit of baby in her voice.

"Hi, my beautiful girl. It's your mommy!"

"Hi, Mommy. I'm bored." The dreaded word every parent hates to hear. "And I miss you, Mom!"

"I miss you, too, Stinky. You're not having fun anymore?"

"I am, but it's hot here and the bugs are really really big! I miss my toys an' stuff and the food's kind of icky."

That's not a good way to impress the relatives I never see: have my city kid bashing the "country" life.

"Okay, sweetie, not so loud! Let me talk to Gramma. You'll be home soon. I love you and I miss you so much."

"Love you, too! GRAMMA. MOMMY WANTS YOU!" I think my ear started to bleed.

"Hello?"

"Hi, Mom. What's goin' on there? Sarah's not having a good time anymore?"

"She's fine. I think she just misses you."

"Well, I miss her, too. Maybe just a little while longer, huh? I really miss you guys."

"They're planning a big barbecue in a couple of days. It would be a shame to miss that. Why don't you just check back in tomorrow?"

"Okay. Ahh!" I swerved as someone cut me off. "I'll talk to you guys tomorrow!"

By the time I got home, I was famished. Unfortunately, there wasn't much in the fridge, so I pulled out a frozen mac and cheese dinner and nuked it. At least it was organic! And low in preservatives, high in cheesy fat. I poured a nice pinot grigio into a fancy wineglass and took a big sip. That made me feel more civilized.

I took out the piece of paper with Aaron Summers's parents' address on it and set it on the table. They lived in Hancock Park, California. That was only about five minutes from Aaron's place. Why had they asked to have his things shipped? The real question was, What reason could I have to drive over there and talk to them? Or what reason could I invent? The landlady hadn't said anything about giving the address to the police, so probably what I should do is call Jakes and pass it on to him.

Thinking about Jakes, I remembered what his partner had said to me in the parking lot. Were Frank Jakes's feelings for me so strong that he was putting his job on the line? And if he did feel strongly about me, how did I feel about him? Paul was going to be gone until the end of the month. That gave me almost two weeks to figure it out.

I grabbed the phone and dialed Jakes's cell number before I realized that I had memorized it.

"Hello?"

For some reason I almost froze, almost hung up, but finally said, "Uh, hello, Jakes. It's—"

"Alex," he said, "hi."

"Hi."

"What can I do for you?"

"Did I catch you at work?"

"No, you actually caught me in my car leaving work," he said. "Where are you?"

"I'm . . . home."

"Is something wrong?"

"I don't know," I said. "Is there?"

He hesitated and then asked, "What is it, Alex? What's on your mind?"

"Your partner came to see me today, at work," I said. "I mean . . . well, in the parking lot at work." I was aware that I was stammering, and I didn't know why.

"Uh-huh."

"He had, uh, something he wanted to tell me . . . about you."

"Okay, let me stop you right there, Alex," he said. "I'd rather not do this over the phone."

"Oh, uh, okay . . ."

"Can we meet somewhere . . . or can I come there?" he asked.

"Um, here?"

"Yes," he said. "I thought you said your daughter was with your mother? On a trip?"

"That's right."

"And Paul . . . he's out of town?"

Somehow I could sense where he was going with this. I hesitated. "Yes."

"So . . . can we meet and talk?"

No, I thought. "Yes," I said.

"Be there in a few."

Chapter 20

He rang the bell and I let him in.

"Want some coffee?" I asked.

"Coffee? Are we planning on being up all night?" I looked at him and he held my eyes. "How about something a little stronger?" He picked up a purple My Little Pony. "Nice hair."

"That's my daughter's. I have an opened bottle of white wine."

"Yeah, I figured it was Sarah's. Nothing stronger?"

I smiled at him questioningly. This was kind of feeling like a dare. Or maybe it was just my competitive nature.

"Sorry, I'm all out of rotgut. Have a seat." I pulled out another wineglass and got mine from the sink.

He sat at the table and looked out the back door at the canals.

"This brings back some fond memories." He was referring to last year when I had been saved from a much too near death experience by him and Paul. "Suppose you tell me what's on your mind, Alex?"

"Let's talk about you first."

He took a sip—no, make that a gulp—of wine.

"What about me?" he asked. "What did my partner tell you?"

"He said you were getting yourself into trouble."

"That's nothing new," he said. "Did he say why this time?"

"Yes, he said it was . . . because of me."

"You?"

"Yes," I said, "me."

We stared at each other across the table. He picked up a strawberry from a bowl on the table and popped it in his mouth. "Did he say what he meant?"

"I think you know what he meant, Jakes." I bit into a strawberry and slowly chewed it. He was staring at my mouth. And I was staring at him staring at my mouth. Jeez! What was this turning into—*9½ Weeks*?

"Look," Jakes said, "I don't know how deep you want to get into this right now, Alex."

I couldn't tell if he was kidding or what exactly. "To tell you the truth"—and I was—"neither am I. Why don't we stick to talking about how much trouble you're in because of me?"

"None," he said. "Any trouble I'm in is always my own doing. You just let me worry about it." He went for another strawberry and slowly bit into it. Juice was running down his chin. He brushed it away with the back of his hand, looking at me the whole time. Was he doing this on purpose?

"Would you please just stop it?"

"Stop what?"

"You know what. The whole biting into the strawberry thing . . . The juice."

He popped another one into his mouth. "I have no idea what you're talking about. These are good. Where did you get them? Whole Foods?" He was lying, but I couldn't prove it so I went back to the topic at hand.

"You've been giving me special treatment, haven't you? Not considering me a suspect? Letting me help?"

"You know things about these people I don't," he explained. "And I'm not treating you as a suspect because I don't consider you one."

"Even though everyone else who was there that day at the Emmys *is* a suspect."

"Were," Jakes said. "They were suspects in the beginning. I didn't know them. I know you."

Then I had to go and open my big fat mouth. "Well, I found out something today, as a matter of fact."

"What's that?"

I couldn't help myself. I was excited about the info. I told him about visiting Aaron Summers's landlady and getting his parents' address from her.

"What the hell are you doing? It really bugs me that you do that kind of thing on your own. You're an actress, remember? I'm the detective." He gave me a stern look and then asked, "Why did you start with Summers?"

"He auditioned for a role on my old soap. I was able to get his home address and check it out."

"Well, four are actors," he answered. "I checked with the Screen Actors Guild and AFTRA, like you suggested."

"Four?" I asked. "What about the fifth man?"

"Still checking."

I sat back in my chair. "Jakes, if they're all actors, what does this mean?"

"Somebody's obviously targeting actors, but it's a little more than that."

We weren't including Henri in our conversation. He had not been an actor. He was the square peg in the round hole.

"How do you mean?"

"They're all the same type," he said. "Young, handsome studs, from what I've been able to find out. Not look-alikes, but the same general type."

"So it's not bad enough that somebody may be targeting soap actors, but they're picking a certain type."

"Right."

"So, does this mean you have a serial killer?"

Jakes winced and said, "My boss doesn't want to hear that term, but if I find that the fifth man was an actor, then, yes, that's what my report is going to have to say. Except for one thing."

"What's that?"

"Well, if you hadn't recognized Aaron Summers's picture, we might not have known they were actors. I mean, it's not like they were making their living at it. They all had other jobs, except for Jackson Masters."

"But they have worked as actors."

"To some extent," he said. "A couple of them had done commercials, local plays, that kind of thing. Jackson was the only one who was actually working on a show at the time of his death. And I still have to find out about the fifth man."

"When will you know?"

"Tomorrow," he said. "Len's supposed to be working that angle, but I guess he took some time off to talk to you."

"He cares about you."

"Sure," Jakes said. "Me and his job. If I get in trouble, he doesn't want any of it getting on him."

"I don't understand," I said. "I thought partners were very close—"

"We haven't been able to do that," he said. "Len replaced my old partner, whom I was with for twelve years. Even though Len and I have been together for five, there's just this . . . space between us."

"What happened to him? Your old partner?"

"He . . . died."

"Oh," I said. "I'm sorry. Was he killed in the line of duty?"

"Yeah," Jakes said.

"I'm sorry," I said again. I was waiting for him to elaborate, but it was obviously a sore subject. "I won't pry. . . . I mean it's not like we're really close. . . ."

He just nodded. "You got that address for me?"

"I'd like to go with you to see the parents."

"Why?"

"Because I was there when Jackson was killed," I said.

He sat back in his chair. "I can't take you."

"Why not?"

"You're too recognizable, Alex," he said, "especially to a family whose son was part of your world, even on a part-time basis."

"I don't understand the problem."

"You'd be a distraction," he said. "Didn't you tell me the woman you talked to today kept gushing?"

"Yes, but she still came up with the address, didn't she?"

He smiled and said, "An address you haven't given me yet."

After I handed it to him, I walked him to the front door. We walked close together, occasionally brushing against each other. I didn't know if he was doing it, or I was, or if it was a combination of both.

We stood in the doorway.

"So," he said, "what's going on? I'm not leaving until you tell me."

I was sort of stuck between the wall and his chest. Very close. I tried to look away but he held my chin and looked me in the eyes.

"Let me help you. I know you need someone to listen."

I was desperately trying not to cry. But despite my best efforts, a tear slid down my cheek.

"I'm sorry. I don't know why this is so fucking hard for me. . . . I hate putting this on you," I stammered.

"I want you to put it on me, Alex. I want you to. Let me help."

I just looked at him, blinking back my tears. I surrendered. "It's my ex-husband. Sarah's father. I never told you. He embezzled some money from me years ago and then took off. I haven't heard from him since. Until a few weeks ago. He called to say he was coming back to the States and wanted to see Sarah. That piece of shit!"

"How is that a bad thing?" he asked. "You can press charges, maybe get some of that money back."

"He wants to see Sarah," I said again, and then I added, "He threatened me."

"Why would he threaten you? Did you provoke him in some way?" He had shifted into cop gear.

"Hell, yeah, I provoked him. He can't just stroll back into our lives like nothing ever happened. He's a sonofabitch motherfucker! And I told him so."

"Do you think he would ever try to hurt you? Did he ever abuse you when you were together?"

"Never physically. His was a more subtle psychological kind of abuse." I sighed. "I don't know who he is anymore. Maybe he's desperate. I don't know what to do." I started sobbing.

"It's okay. Give me his name and I'll talk to the Feds to see if his passport has been active. I'll track him down one way or another." He looked at me like he knew what I was thinking. "Sarah will be fine—don't worry. I'll make sure of it."

"How are you going to do that?" I asked him a little skeptically.

"When are they due back?" he asked.

"In a couple of days."

"I'll make sure she has someone following her. All the time. Everywhere."

"You can do that? Without getting into more trouble?" That's all he needed was more flack from upstairs because of me.

"Don't worry about it. People owe me favors. Enough said," he answered when I tried to interrupt.

"Thanks. That means a lot. Okay, then." I looked at him gratefully. We were so close I could smell his breath. It smelled sweet like strawberries. I was looking down and then looked up to meet his bluer than blue eyes.

He reached out his right hand and touched my mouth. His fingers moved from my lips to my cheek. I don't know what he meant to do—stroke my cheek and leave, maybe—but suddenly his hand went behind my neck and he was drawing me forward with strong but not forceful pressure, his eyes holding mine the whole time. I could have stopped, but I didn't, and when our lips touched it was too late.

He tasted like strawberries, too.

Chapter 21

He was a good kisser. And he kept doing it. He had his hands around my waist, firmly but not too firmly. You'd think he'd want to move them up or down or into more interesting territory, but he seemed content to just leave them there and keep kissing me. Slowly and deeply. He took one of his hands and moved it to the small of my back, gently pressing me toward him a little. I could feel every part of his body, and he was muscular in all the right places. I put my hands on his butt. Yep. Muscular there, too. Then he started kissing my face. All over. Sweet, sexy kisses that trailed from my forehead to my cheeks and down to my neck. He was taking his time. It could have been an hour, but I think it was a minute. I even forgot where I was.

Then it kind of dawned on me that I had a boyfriend. He must have sensed what I was thinking because he gently stopped. He didn't pull away. I was breathless and a little self-conscious. He was looking at me with such an earnest expression, it was disconcerting.

"Aren't you going to say something?" I asked after a few seconds.

"What is there to say?"

"I don't know. I mean . . . there's Paul and everything. This isn't right." I was stammering and not proud of it.

"Yeah. It *feels* right, though, doesn't it?" It wasn't really a question. More a statement of fact.

I couldn't argue with him. It really did. Our lips were almost touching as we spoke, and his breath stilled smelled like strawberries. His beard was a little scratchy, too, but in a good way. I was dying to kiss him again, but instead I said, "I've got some thinking and sorting out to do."

"Yes, you do," he said simply. I thought he would go in for another kiss. I was hoping, anyway, but he gently took his hands away from around my waist and opened the door.

"By the way, don't worry about me and my job, okay? I'm a big boy. In fact, you're not bringing anything into my life I don't want right now."

I wished I could say the same to him. I wasn't sure what I wanted and that was the problem. He started toward his car and then I thought of something. "Are you heading out to see Aaron's family tomorrow?"

He turned back to me. "Yeah. I'll be at work and then go over in the late morning. Why, Alex?" he asked me pointedly.

"Just wondering!"

He looked at me skeptically. "You have a good night. And don't worry about your ex. I'll handle it. I've got it covered." He turned and got into his car. I wanted to run after him, jump on him and kiss his sweet face, but instead I nodded and closed the door. I felt something sticky on my upper lip and licked it off. Strawberries.

*   *   *

Later, with a warm feeling inside, I called George.

"What's up, sweetie?" he asked.

"This time," I said, "I *am* in trouble."

George chuckled and said, "That's what I wanted to hear!"

It's nice to have friends.

George told me to come right over for martinis and gossip. I went, even though I knew I was to be the subject of the gossip.

"It'll be just us," he said, indicating that Wayne would be there, too.

When I got there George answered the door and let me in with a hug. We went into the living room where Wayne—with impeccable timing—was putting a tray of martini glasses and a shaker on the table. "Some trendy things aren't worth the time of day. Chocolate martinis aren't one of them!" He shook that shaker and poured a mocha-looking liquid into a glass and handed it to me.

I had died and gone to heaven! This was actually what I needed. Friendly faces, sympathetic ears and the most deliciously decadent martini the world could ever know. A woman with PMS must have invented these!

"I know I'm crazy," I told them, licking chocolate off my lip "but . . . the detective stuff, it's exciting, you know?"

Wayne poked me. "And so is the detective, right?"

"Leave it to Wayne to get right to the point!" George laughed.

"I'm not wasting these martinis on chitchat! Let's talk about the juicy stuff! Are you going to see him again?"

"Well . . . yeah. I'm helping with the investigation. Or I was."

"What happened?" George asked.

"He thinks I'm too recognizable to go along when he talks to the families of the victims."

"Why? Do they watch the show?" Wayne asked.

"All the dead men auditioned for one soap or another," I said, "so, yeah, maybe."

"If I know you, Alex," George said, "you're not going to let a little something like that stop you."

He was right. I already had an idea for the next day.

"Can I ask you a question, sweetie?" George asked.

"Sure." I was a little wary of what he wanted to know, though.

"What do you think you would be doing if Paul wasn't in your life?"

"What would I be doing?" I repeated. "You mean where Jakes is concerned?" They both nodded. "I don't know. We might be involved somewhat. Who's to say?"

"Who are you trying to kid? This man is gorgeous, he's sexy and he has a major thing for you. So what's stopping you?" Wayne was getting impatient with me.

"Wayne," George said, "what Alex needs from us is not pressure. She needs us to listen and to just . . . be here."

"With chocolate martinis," I added, pouring another. "These are good."

"They *are* good," Wayne said. With an enigmatic smile Wayne added, "But hunky detectives are better."

Chapter 22

I went to Parker Center the next morning and asked for Detective Frank Jakes.

"Can I say what it's about, ma'am?" the sergeant asked.

"Murder," I said.

"Who's been murdered?"

"The detective is working on several murders," I said. "I have some information that might help him."

He looked me up and down curiously. I pushed my glasses up my nose with my forefinger and stared at him.

"Please have a seat, ma'am," he said. "I'll tell the detective you're here."

"Thank you."

I sort of waddled over to a seat and sat down. When I looked up, he was still staring at me. I was hoping it wasn't because he recognized me. He looked away quickly when I caught him.

Several minutes later Jakes showed up. He spoke to the sergeant, who pointed at me. Jakes looked over with a puzzled expression and then joined me. I stood and pushed the glasses up again.

"Ma'am?" he said. "Can I help you?"

"You are Detective Jakes?" I asked with a hint of a Southern accent.

"Yes."

"You're older than I thought you'd be."

He seemed mildly amused. "I'm sorry to hear that," he said. "The sergeant says you have information about the murders I'm working on?"

"Yes," I said. "The actors."

"Actors?"

"The soap actors who have been killed."

Any semblance of amusement left his face. I knew he hadn't released information that he was working on more than one murder or that all the victims were actors. He was wondering how I knew. And he was wondering who the heck I was.

"Now, ma'am, how would you know anything about that?" he asked.

"What's the matter, Detective?" I asked in my own voice. "Is absolutely nothing about me familiar to you?"

He stared at me, narrowing his eyes, actually leaned forward to look at my face, and then said, "Alex?"

"I told you I'm playing twins on my show. One of them looks quite different from me—I hope so, anyway." I turned away from him and took the false teeth out of my mouth. "See?"

"Is that a phony nose?" he asked with a wicked gleam in his eye.

"No, it's not! Smart-ass." I poked his stomach with my finger. "That's all mine. I added the teeth, glasses, contact lenses, gray wig, some body padding and a little bit of a Southern accent. What do you think?"

"I think it's amazing," he said. Despite the getup, I

could tell he was happy to see me. "Are you trying to impress me with your acting talents, because if you are, it's really not necessary."

"Just listen. I want to go with you when you interview the families," I said, "and I just proved they won't recognize me. Especially Jackson's family."

"Well, won't they recognize your character from your new show?" Jakes said.

"This was just for your benefit. I know you don't watch my show. I'll put on a different wig and mess around with my makeup. They'll never know." I got a little closer to him. I wasn't above using feminine wiles when it served my purposes. On occasion, I mean.

"So, what do you think?" He didn't smell like strawberries anymore but was still worth a good long sniff.

He sighed. I could tell he was torn. He wanted to be with me and this was as good an excuse as any. I felt the same way.

"All right. Just make a few alterations, though nothing . . . this drastic."

"I can use the ladies' room—"

"No," he said, "not here. We'll stop by your car so you can pick up your things. You can change on the way."

He took my elbow and led me out of the room and down a hallway.

"In the car?" I asked doubtfully. "Can't I go home?"

"No, it's out of the way," he said. "We'll find a place along the way."

"Hey, Jakes," somebody yelled, "the boss wants to see you!"

"Say you just missed me!" he called back.

"But—"

We kept walking.

"Don't you want to—"

"No," he said. "My boss will tie me up for hours. Let's just go—we'll take the stairs. . . ."

He rushed me to his car in the parking lot and then drove us to mine to pick up my makeup kit and extra clothes. Then he took me to a restaurant he knew had a large ladies' room.

"And don't ask me how I know," he said as we went in. "I'll wait at the bar."

Chapter 23

When I came back to the bar, Jakes was sitting with an iced tea in front of him and another waiting for me. He looked at me blankly, and then it registered that it was me.

"Jeez! You look completely different again!"

"I know! Isn't it so cool?" I was having way too much fun with this.

"One question. Why are all your disguises so un-attractive? Don't you have any with, say, a platinum blond wig and big boobs, maybe a miniskirt?" he asked with a sexy smile.

"Maybe I do, maybe I don't!" I felt flustered again. Why did he do that to me? "Now, seriously, why are you ducking your boss? And how come you're never with your partner?"

"Look," he said, "I'm having some trouble at work, but it's got nothing to do with you. I don't like my boss, and I don't get along with my partner. He and I have agreed to work on this case separately."

"You've agreed?"

"Yes," he said. "I got confirmation from him that yes, the fifth dead man was also an actor."

"Wait, wait," I said. "Let's not get off this subject so fast."

"What subject?"

"The subject of you and your partner and work—"

"Alex," he said, starting to sound exasperated, "I had a life before I met you. You have to believe that this has nothing to do with you."

"Okay," I said. "So do you think this will work?" I gestured to my disguise, turned toward him and framed my face with my hands.

"You look . . . severe," he said. "Like a librarian."

"That's the point," I said. "And I have these."

I took out a pair of large plastic-framed glasses and put them on.

"Okay," he said, "nobody will recognize you in that getup."

"How do we introduce me?"

"You'll be my associate," he said. "I'm not gonna to tell anyone that you're a cop."

"Okay, I see your point," I said. "The last time I helped you solve a case, you called me your consultant. Am I being promoted or demoted?"

He looked at me blankly. "Just don't speak. I ask all the questions."

"What if I think of a question—?"

He cut me off with a look.

"Okay, you're right. I'll just sit quietly, take a few notes and look like an associate. Whatever the hell that is."

We got up and started out the door. A little bitter but happy to be going along, I shut my mouth and followed him to the car, noticing what a nice butt he had.

Chapter 24

The families lived spread out over the greater Los Angeles area, starting with Aaron's family in Hancock Park. I had no idea whether we could get all the questioning done in one day. In the car, Jakes reminded me of the names of the other three men who were killed. They were Kyle Hansen, Tom Nolan and Mason Stone. Mason Stone? It was hard for me to believe parents could be so cruel. That had to be a stage name. Or a porn name. Is that the same thing?

"How many interviews are we doing today?" I asked.

"We're going to try to do the three in Southern California," he said. "One of the others has family up in Northern California. Len is going to travel to do that one."

"And the fifth?"

"Canada," he said. "We're going to do that one by phone. If we think it needs something more we'll call the locals. If we're still not satisfied, then Len or I will go up there."

"So we only have three."

"Yes," he said, "and hopefully we'll be able to get

them all done today. But if not, we'll finish up tomorrow. When do you have to go back to work?"

"Tomorrow. But I have a lot of dialogue. It will take me some time to learn all my lines."

"It sounds kind of like homework."

"It is! Just as tedious sometimes, too. I have a pretty decent memory, though, so it's easier for me to memorize lines than for a lot of the other actors."

He looked at me out of the corner of his eye. "I bet you were good in school, right? Teacher's pet, cheerleader? Huh?"

"Well, yeah . . . I've been known to put on a skirt and sweater and grab a pom-pom. And yes, I was on the honor roll a couple of times. Why? You got something against smart cheerleaders?"

"Not at all. I just didn't run in that crowd. In fact I tried to avoid school as much as possible."

"Really? I would have pegged you as someone who was good at school."

"I probably would have been. Too many distractions, though."

"But you managed to get through," I said. "High school? College?"

"College," he said. "You have to have a degree to get into most police departments now. I managed to get my degree at night."

"Degree?"

"Criminal justice," he said. "A minor in law."

"Did you want to be a lawyer?"

"Hell, no," he said. "I just wanted to know what I was talking about."

"And do you?"

He looked at me quickly and then put his eyes back

on the road. "When it comes to my job," he answered, "yes."

So far neither of us had brought up what happened the night before. I assumed he was referring to that but I wasn't completely sure. I really didn't know how to even approach talking about it.

So I didn't. I mean it was just a kiss, right?

"Do you have any theories?" I asked.

"About what?"

"Motives for these murders," I said. "They can't be isolated, right?"

"No," he said. "We're working on the assumption that the murders are connected."

"So someone has it in for good-looking young actors."

"Apparently."

"Like whom?"

"You tell me," he said. "Give me some possibilities . . . a theory."

"Oh, okay."

When I didn't speak right away, he said, "You must have given it some thought before now."

"Well, yes . . ."

"So?"

"Girlfriends?"

"More than one?"

"Sure," I said. "What if all of the men went out with the same girl—or girls? Say two? Maybe three?"

"And these guys didn't call again? The woman—or women—killed the bastards? Are females really that angry? Really?"

"Sometimes. Okay, maybe not," I said.

"Well, somebody has to be pissed enough to kill them and string them up."

"They were all . . . hanged?"

He risked another look at me and then back to the road. I noticed he was a very good driver.

"Do you really want to know all the details, Alex?" he asked. "All the . . . gory details?"

"What do you think?" I looked at him. "Just think of me the way you would Detective Davis."

He flashed me a sexy grin and said, "Trust me, that ain't gonna happen."

Chapter 25

We were in the living room of a small house deep in the San Fernando Valley. It was a middle-class residential area where one of the young men, Tom Nolan, grew up.

Jakes told me he had not called ahead. He never liked to warn people that he was going to be questioning them, not even the family members of the deceased.

"You don't suspect the families." It wasn't a question.

"Not in this case, but you never know what you can learn by surprising people."

So we surprised Nolan's mother, who let us in when Jakes showed her his ID. As planned, he introduced me as his "associate." She didn't ask any questions.

She showed us into the small, neat living room and said her husband was at work. She could call him if we wanted her to.

"That won't be necessary," Jakes said. "We just have some questions about Tom's death. We're sorry to intrude, but—"

"Have you taken over his case?" she asked. She

sat on the sofa and rubbed her arms as if she were suddenly cold. She was as neat and well taken care of as the room. Not expensively dressed or made-up, but she apparently knew how to use her clothes and makeup to show herself off to her best advantage. Her hair was black as coal. I was sure it was dyed, but it was a good dye job, making her look younger than she was, which was probably early fifties. Her body showed she spent time at a gym.

"Yes, ma'am, we have," Jakes said. "We believe that whoever killed Tom has also killed at least four other young men around the same age, so we're consolidating all the cases."

Her eyes widened. She looked from Jakes to me and then back. "You mean my son was killed by a serial killer?"

"We haven't put a label to the killer yet, Mrs. Nolan," he said.

"My name is Sadowski," she said. "Tom changed his name to Nolan for his acting."

"Sorry," Jakes said. "Mrs. Sadowski, did Tom work much as an actor?"

"On and off," she said. "He always told us when he was going to be in something. H-he hadn't booked anything in a while."

I stood and listened as Jakes continued to ask questions. Watching him only confirmed what I already suspected to be true—he was very good at his job. I guess last year, when he was questioning me, I was too busy to notice. He asked her things I knew he had the answers to, but they always seemed to set up another question he needed answered. He had a way with women, was very good putting them at ease, but I knew that much already, didn't I?

"Mrs. Sadowski—" he started, but she stopped him.

"Just call me Margie, okay? It's better than Missus. Makes me feel so . . . old."

"Okay, Margie," he said. "Did Tom ever tell you that he'd been threatened by anyone? Or did he have a fight with anyone?"

"I told the other detectives, Tom didn't fight. He was . . . gentle. People liked him. I can't think of anyone who'd do this to him. I've wracked my brain for just one reason."

"And your husband?"

"He doesn't know anything—he knows less about Tom than I do. They didn't . . . get along. Not since Tom quit law school to act."

"Your husband is a lawyer?"

"Yes," she said. "Corporate. He has his own firm, a small one. He had dreams of Tom working with him. He's very bitter—*was* very bitter—that it never happened."

"What about you, Margie?"

"What do you mean?" She looked at me. I kept my librarian's face blank.

"Are you bitter? About anything?"

"Well . . . yeah," she said, looking at him like he was crazy. She hugged herself tighter. "I'm bitter about losing my son."

"Do you have any other children?"

"No." She looked in my direction again and this time spoke to me. "Do you have a cigarette? I'm trying to quit." She wrung her hands and then shook them out. "Don't know what to do with my hands."

"I'm sorry," I said. "I don't smoke."

She looked at Jakes.

"Sorry."

"It's becoming such a nonsmoking world," she complained.

Jakes asked a few more questions, thanked her and then asked for the address of her husband's office. After that we left.

"You're very good at this," I said, in the car.

"Does that surprise you?"

"No," I said. "I've been on the receiving end of your questions, remember?"

"I've been doing it for a long time." He started the car.

"Are we going to see the husband now?"

"No," he said. "We'll go see Aaron Summers's folks."

"Why not the husband?"

"Because she'll call him now and he'll be waiting for us," he answered. "I want to talk to him when he's not expecting us."

"Tomorrow?"

"Probably."

He put the car in drive and pulled away from the curb.

Chapter 26

Aaron Summers's parents lived in a much more up-scale neighborhood than Tom Nolan's, in an area adjacent to Hollywood called Hancock Park. Gorgeous homes built in the twenties and thirties. Unfortunately, it's surrounded by a not so nice section of Hollywood. We had to wait at the front gate while Jakes identified himself and then drive up a circular driveway, where he parked behind a Lexus and a big yellow Hummer.

We were let in by a maid who walked us through the house and out back by a pool, where Mr. and Mrs. Summers were sitting, both in bathing suits.

"Detective . . . ," the man said.

"Jakes."

"And?" He looked at me. Were we going to get away with this again?

"My associate," Jakes said.

The man waited, and when Jakes didn't say anything else he asked, "What can we do for you and your associate, Detective Jakes?"

I looked at the woman I assumed was his wife. She had bleached blond hair, big dark glasses and fake boobs of the Pamela Anderson variety on a toned body barely covered by a bikini. Does everybody in LA live at the gym but me? Apparently so. She was about thirty. I suddenly realized this couldn't be Aaron's mother. Probably wife number two—or more.

Her husband was a direct contrast to her, about thirty years older. The black hair on his flabby chest and portly stomach was wet with perspiration, as was his bald dome.

I looked at Jakes. He was staring straight at Mr. Summers. I admired his dedication to duty and the fact that he wasn't mesmerized by the double Ds.

"We're here to talk to you about your son, Aaron," Jakes said.

"Talk to his mother, not me."

"Why not you?"

"He and I hadn't talked for a long time before he . . . died."

"He didn't just die, Mr. Summers," Jakes said. "Somebody killed him."

"Same thing."

"No," Jakes said, "it's not the same thing. Frankly, I'm a little disappointed by your attitude, Mr. Summers."

"Well, I was very disappointed in Aaron," the man said.

Was this the same situation as with Tom Nolan's father? I wondered. Father disappointed in son's choice of career? Did this happen with daughters, too? I thought about Sarah and wondered what she would decide to do for a career, and how I'd feel about it. Short of her taking up lap dancing, I doubted I'd have a problem with whatever she chose to do.

"You didn't approve of his career?"

"That acting thing? That's not a career," the man said. "That's a joke. You know how many parts he's had in six years? Two. And a million auditions he never got called back for."

"That's the business," Jakes said.

"It's his mother's fault," Summers said. "She encouraged him."

"When's the last time you saw your son, Mr. Summers?" Jakes asked.

"Months ago. He came to borrow money."

"You didn't give it to him, did you?"

"Bingo."

"And is this Mrs. Summers?" Jakes asked, looking at the woman in the bikini.

"It is."

"We're newlyweds," she gushed, speaking for the first time. "We got married last week."

"Congratulations," Jakes said. "Have you ever met Aaron?"

"Never. I wanted to, though. So sad. I was looking forward to being a stepmommy. I've seen pictures. He was very cute. Just like his dad." She wrapped herself around her new husband and bit his earlobe.

"She doesn't know anything about him," Summers said, pushing her away. "Hey, look, I told this to the other cops."

"Well, now you're telling it to me," Jakes said. "I've got a few more questions. . . ."

After about half a dozen more questions Jakes said, "By the way, Mr. Summers, what do you do for a living?"

"I'm a producer."

That surprised both Jakes and me.

"And you have such a low opinion of acting?" Jakes asked.

"And actors."

"Well, not *all* actors. I'm an actor, er, actress," Mrs. Summers said proudly. "That's how we met."

Summers just looked at Jakes and said, "Is that all?"

Jakes closed the pad he'd been using to jot down notes. "I may need to talk to you again, Mr. Summers."

"Like I said," Summers replied, "talk to his mother. And his landlady. She probably knew more about him than I did."

"We'll do that. Don't worry."

We didn't speak until we got in the car and closed the door.

"Why do these people—both parents we spoke to today—have such a low opinion of actors?" Jakes asked.

"I think it's the profession," I said, "not the individuals."

"Okay," he said, "why the profession?"

"You have to be crazy to be an actor, Jakes," I said. "I thought you'd know that after being in your job all these years. I mean, you've dealt with crazy actors before, right?"

He grinned. "Present company excepted?"

"Oh," I said, "no."

Chapter 27

"None of these victims were married?" I asked as we drove to the home of Jackson Masters's parents.

"No, none of them," Jakes said. "At least, not as far as we know. I talked with people they worked with already."

"That's right," I said. "They weren't full-time actors. What else did they do?"

"Aaron Summers was a bartender," Jakes said. "Very popular with the ladies. Wasn't unusual for him to end up going home with someone on any given night. Or day, from what I've heard."

"What about Tom Nolan?"

"Waiter," Jakes said. "Food service seems to be a big day job for you actors. At the time of his death he was working at a café in Hollywood. Same story. The other waiters and waitresses said he was a ladies' man."

"And we know Jackson was."

"Right."

"And the other two?"

"Len's checking on the fifth one," Jakes said. "We'll

have to wait for the police in Toronto to get back to us."

"Mounties?"

"I don't know," Jakes said. "Apparently there are some provinces up there that have their own police."

We drove in silence for a while, a silence that became awkward. Apparently neither one of us was ready yet to talk about last night. Granted, it was just a kiss, but then again we both knew it was more. I felt bad about Paul.

"Do we know if any of them were gay?" I asked.

"No."

"We could have asked the families today."

"Those families? Forget it. If any of them were gay, it will come up in the investigation eventually." He snorted. "Imagine that last guy finding out his kid was gay?"

"You're right," I said. "He wouldn't have taken that very well. What about forensics?"

"What about it?"

"Do you have anything from any of the crime scenes?" I asked. "Fibers? Fingerprints?"

"You know, I forgot that you have an interest in that sort of thing. How did that start?"

"I got hooked on mystery novels at a young age and then true crime books several years ago," I said, "and then I discovered Court TV—or truTV, as they call it now. And as it got bigger on TV—*48 Hours*, all the A&E shows—I just got more and more interested."

"Well, I have to say you're a pretty good amateur detective," he said.

"Can't say I've done much amateur detecting in this case."

"Well, forensics hasn't come up with much for us,"

Jakes said. "But I'm still a firm believer in footwork and real intuitive detective work."

"Which is what you do?"

"It's what I've always done," he said, "and it's what I respect. I think you have some of that in you, Alex. You know what questions to ask."

"Well . . . thank you."

I didn't know if he was saying that because he believed it or because he liked me. I decided I'd be able to figure that out for myself eventually.

There was silence again, and this time he broke it. "You ever meet Jackson's folks?"

"Once," I said. "They came to a Christmas party at the studio. It meant a lot to him to have them there. He wanted to impress them."

"Well, then," he said, "I guess we're about to find out just how good your disguise is."

I wasn't sure if they'd remember me from when we last met or recognize me from watching the show.

I hadn't gone real heavy with makeup for the librarian look. Jakes was right. We were going to find out how good my disguise was.

Jackson Masters's family was middle class. The house was in Culver City, predominately known for its multitude of movie and TV studios: MGM, now Sony, Fox, et cetera. It was a small and well-cared-for home. I wondered if they would care as much about their son. I hadn't spent that much time with them at the Christmas party, but as we approached the house I was nervous about being recognized.

A woman answered when Jakes rang the doorbell. Seeing him, she tried patting her graying hair into place. "Yes?"

"Mrs. Masters. My name is Detective Jakes. This is my associate . . ."

The woman looked at me expectantly.

I said the first name that came to mind. "Tiffany. I'm a consultant."

What an idiot I am! Tiffany was the name of the character I used to play on *The Yearning Tide*. That's the only name I could think of? Luckily, she didn't seem to take much notice.

"Is this about Jackson's murder?" she asked, looking at Jakes again.

"Yes, ma'am. Is Mr. Masters home?"

"Yes, he is," she said. "We've just finished dinner and were going to have some coffee and cake. Would you like some?"

This was our third interview of the day, and we hadn't stopped for lunch. I tried to send Jakes a mental message that I wanted cake.

"That would be nice, ma'am."

"Please don't call me that, Detective," she said. "My name is Charlotte. Follow me."

She led us down a hall to a small kitchen. There was a man seated at the table, which was covered with remnants of what looked like a meat loaf dinner. Such wholesomeness made it clear that these people must have been originally from the Midwest.

"Dear, these are the police," she said. "They're here about Jackson."

Jackson's father had possibly the saddest eyes I'd ever seen.

"Have you found his killer?" he asked us.

"No, sir," Jakes said. "Not yet."

"Honey, would you take Detective Jakes and Tiffany . . ." She left it hanging.

I hesitated and said, "Lamp—Lampis." My God, I am the worst!

Jakes shot me a look of incredulity but it seemed to go over the Masterses' heads.

". . . Tiffany Lampis into the dining room? I'll bring the coffee and cake in there."

"All right."

The man stood and walked out without a word.

"He's still very distraught," she said. "Just follow him, and, please, don't ask him any questions until I join you. He's . . . not well."

"All right, Charlotte," Jakes said with a smile.

We followed in Mr. Masters's wake and found him sitting at the dining room table.

"You look familiar," Jackson's father said to me.

"Really?" I gulped.

"Yes," he said. He dropped it, thankfully.

Charlotte Masters came in carrying a tray of coffee and what looked like a marble cake. "We've spoken before, Detective, haven't we?" she asked.

"Yes, briefly. But we're pursuing some . . . a new direction."

She put the tray down on the table, inviting us to get comfortable. I sat across from her, while Jakes sat across from her husband, who seemed to have gone somewhere inside himself.

"My husband suffered a stroke last year," she told us, putting her hand on his. "He hasn't fully recovered his mental capacities and probably never will. He understands about Jackson, though."

"Jackson's dead," the older man said. He looked at me. "Somebody killed my son."

"Yes, sir," I said, "and we're going to find out who did it."

A tear rolled down his cheek and then just as suddenly he looked at his wife and asked, "Is there cake?"

She poured him a cup of coffee and gave him a small plate with a piece of cake on it. "Be careful, Bill," she said. "The coffee's hot. Don't burn your mouth."

"I'm not an idiot!" he snapped harshly.

She smiled, rubbed his hand and said, "I know that."

"Mrs. Jackson," Jakes said. "Should we talk somewhere else?"

"No, no, it's fine," she said. "He needs to hear what you have to say."

"All right," he said. "Were you and your husband supportive of your son's acting career?"

"Very much so," she said. "We were very proud of him. We were . . . watching the Emmy show when . . . when it happened."

"Oh, God," I said inadvertently. She looked at me. "I am so sorry. Did you know it was him?"

"Not at the time. We knew something had gone wrong but didn't know exactly what until the police called us." She looked at Jakes. "Was that you?"

"My partner," he said. "Detective Davis."

"Yes," she said, "I recall that name."

"Did you talk to your son often?"

"Every week," she said. "He called every week, especially since Bill's stroke."

"Did he ever say that he was . . . concerned or afraid? Maybe about a stalker or someone who was bothering him?"

"No," she said, "he never said anything like that."

"Do you know any of these names, Charlotte?"

Jakes passed her a list with the other four victims's names on it.

She looked at them and then pushed it back.

"No," she said, "they're not familiar. Would you like some cake?"

I would love some cake, I thought to myself. But that would be impossible with these teeth in my mouth. I had to keep reminding myself they were in there. "No, nothing for me, thanks!"

Chapter 28

"Can I say something?" I asked as we drove away from the Masterses' house. I took my teeth out and placed them in their plastic case.

"Of course."

"It doesn't seem to me we found out all that much today."

"Well, we certainly haven't found out as much as we're going to."

"Meaning?"

"Meaning these were just the initial interviews," he said. "I'll be going back for more."

I frowned. "It seems to me you were pretty thorough when you and your partner questioned me last year."

"That's because you were a suspect," he said. "That day, everybody was a suspect. We had to learn as much as we could before we let you all go."

"I see."

"We did the same at the Kodak Theatre the other night," he said. "We kept everyone who was backstage until we had as much information as we could collect."

He pulled up in front of my house and turned the ignition off.

"Well, thanks for taking me along," I said, "although I'm not sure what good I did."

"Go over your impressions tonight," he said, "and we'll talk tomorrow."

"All right."

I didn't move, or speak. Neither did he.

"Look—" he finally said.

"I think—" I said.

We stopped interrupting each other.

"About last night . . . ," I said, and then stopped on my own.

"Look," he said, "about that . . ."

"It was just a kiss, right?"

"Is that all it was to you?" he asked.

I couldn't think of one intelligent or meaningful thing to say, so I just looked at him like a deer caught in the headlights.

"It's a pretty straightforward question, Alex."

"I've just got to figure some things out, Jakes." I started rubbing my eyes. "I'm sorry. I'm not usually so wishy-washy. I mean, I do care for Paul; it's just—"

"Enough said. Do what you have to do." He seemed to be stifling a yawn, or was it a laugh?

I opened the door and stepped out. "That's okay," I said. "No need to walk me to the door."

"Alex," he said, rolling his window down, "spend a little time going over your impressions of the day. We'll talk tomorrow."

"All right," I said, "tomorrow. By the way, did you find anything out about Randy?"

"I've got it covered. Sarah's safe."

"Thank you," I said simply.

He waited at the curb until I walked inside. I didn't look back.

Once inside I went straight to the kitchen to get some Cheez-Its and a glass of red wine. I was starving. I brought them both into the bathroom and started to remove my makeup. When I looked in the mirror, I gasped. Apparently when I rubbed my eyes during my conversation with Jakes, I had smeared black mascara all over the place. I looked like some crazed raccoon. Not only must Jakes think I'm a wishy-washy flake but an absolutely insane one on top of it. I wanted to cry for several reasons.

"Oh, what the hell." I carried my crackers and wine into the front room and plopped down onto my nice soft pillowed sofa. I needed to get grounded. I needed my daughter. And my mom. And George. Did I need Paul? He definitely wasn't the first person I thought of. Not even in my top three. That obviously meant something. I'd have to make a decision soon, but I couldn't deal with it then, so I decided to go over the day's events in my head.

My impressions? Was that what he'd asked for? Well, it was my impression that I didn't have an impression. Was I really supposed to get something from those interviews? If so, then I was clearly in over my head. Again. I had to admit I was flattered at how willing he was to risk his job to include me in this investigation. And I certainly did not believe him when he said the trouble he was in had nothing to do with me.

I was knee-deep in the investigation of these murders. It started with my knowing Jackson Masters, but now I was very interested in solving all six murders—or the five we knew of so far.

I knew what Gil Grissom would do. (I'd updated my influences from Kojak and Columbo.) On *CSI* he always said, "Follow the evidence." I knew there was a ton of information Jakes had that I didn't. No matter how much he had told me or allowed me to hear, I was still on the outside looking in. What I had to do was either pull myself out of it completely or force him to let me all the way in . . . no matter how much trouble it might make for him.

Like he'd told me earlier in the day, I'd just let him worry about it.

Chapter 29

I woke the next morning with no conflicted feelings. At least, not about the murders. The extent of a personal relationship with Frank Jakes was yet to be determined. But being involved in the murder investigation of six men? I was in for the long haul.

I had spoken with Sarah and my mother before going to bed the night before. I hadn't told my mother everything I was doing, but she sensed something. Whatever reticence she had about leaving the relatives early was resolved. She and Sarah were coming home right after the barbecue the next day. She felt I needed her here and she was right. Since Jakes knew about the Randy thing, I felt a lot better having them both home.

Jakes had said we'd talk today. I didn't know if I was supposed to call him, or he was going to call me. I decided to concern myself with breakfast first, and then get dressed for work. When I was ready and still hadn't heard from him, I decided to go to work and leave making contact up to him.

I had only two scenes to tape that day, but I kept

"going up" on my lines. This is a nice way of saying I was screwing up.

At one point the director called for a break and said, "Get it together, Alex!"

That was for everyone else's benefit, though. During the break he came up to me and asked, "Are you all right, darling?"

His name was Richard Breck. He hated being called "Dick"—so of course we all did. And he called everyone "darling." He'd been directing the show for a couple of years and thought everybody around him bought his on-set tough director act. But he took himself so seriously it was hard for the cast to do the same.

"I'm fine, Dickie," I said. "Just got some things on my mind. I'll get it right this time."

"It's Richard, Alex," he said, gritting his teeth. "And I know you will, hon." He patted my hip awkwardly. "No worries."

"No worries."

We taped the scene, and Dick shouted, "Cut! Brilliant, hon!"

I went to my dressing room and threw on my own clothes. When I came out I saw Dick talking to a young man who—just for a moment—I thought was Jackson Masters.

"Dickie!"

He stopped, turned and looked at me while the young man walked away.

"Alex," he said, "your scenes were fine today—just fine."

"Oh, yeah. Thanks," I said. "Who was that guy you were talking to just now?"

"His name is David something or other," he said. "He's auditioning to replace Jackson."

Well, that explained why he looked so much like Jackson.

"I see," I said. "Thanks."

I walked away from Dick, wondering if I should chase down the guy and warn him that someone was killing actors who looked like him—or like Jackson Masters. Or maybe they all looked like the first actor who was killed. And who was that? I realized that while Jakes had told me the names of the dead actors, I didn't know who had been killed first.

In any case, I thought, maybe I should at least tell the kid to bleach his hair blond.

If he had already auditioned, then he'd been seen by a director—probably not Richard, since I'd been working with him all afternoon—and a producer.

I decided to find out exactly who he was. Maybe then I could get his name and address.

I went upstairs to the production offices and found one of our producers, Sean Peters, sitting behind his desk.

"Sean, did you do an audition today for someone to replace Jackson *already*?"

"Now, don't get upset, Alex," Sean said, smoothing back his gray hair with the palm of one hand. Sean touched his hair whenever a woman entered the room. "We do have to replace Jackson."

"I get that," I said. "I'm just curious. What's his name?"

"The one we saw today is David—" He stopped to look at a piece of paper. "—Eisenstein. Horrible name, but just between you, me and lamppost, we're going to hire him."

"To play Jackson's part."

"Right," Sean said. He stood up—or unfolded. At six-seven he always seemed to unfold when he got to his feet. "I've got to go and talk to Gloria." Gloria Dennis was our head writer. "Was there anything else?"

"No," I said, sitting down. "My damn shoe. I'm just going to take a moment to fix my heel."

"Take as long as you like, Alex." He looked down at me and smoothed his hair again. "See you tomorrow."

"You, too, Sean."

I listened to his steps recede down the hall, and when I couldn't hear them anymore, I quickly sat behind his desk, found a blank piece of paper and copied down David Eisenstein's name, address and vital statistics from his application.

Chapter 30

I was getting into my car at the studio parking lot when I heard "Let's Talk About Sex." Jeez! Caller ID told me it was Detective Jakes.

"I'm sorry," he said right away. "I was shot out of a cannon this morning and haven't had a chance to call. Where are you?"

"I'm leaving work."

"Can you come here?"

"To Parker Center?"

"Yes."

"What for?"

"I can't get away right now," he said, "and I need to talk to you."

"Is anything wrong?"

"Alex . . ."

"Yes, all right," I said. "I was just going to get lunch. . . . Can we eat afterward?"

"Is that all you do? Eat?"

I sighed. "I'm on my way."

I got a pass upstairs with no problem and took the elevator to Jakes's floor at Parker Center. Since I'd been there before, I remembered the way to his office—or his section, or whatever they called it. He didn't have his own office. On TV shows some detectives have offices, but I knew in real life they pretty much just had a desk.

As I entered the room full of desks, I saw his partner, Detective Davis. He spotted me crossing the room toward him.

"Alex," he said.

"Detective Davis, hi. Is Jakes around?"

"He's in with the boss." He indicated a closed door across the room.

"Do you know how long—"

"Don't know," he said. "Why don't you have a seat on that bench? He'll see you when he comes out."

"That bench right by the door?"

"That's the one."

"Thanks."

He nodded. It seemed like he was still mad at me, but I didn't know if it was because I had left *The Yearning Tide* or I was causing problems between him and his partner.

I went and sat down. I could hear the murmur of voices inside, voices that occasionally became agitated. Then suddenly the door opened briefly, but before I could sneak a peek it closed again but not all the way. It was ajar, and I could hear everything.

"You're lettin' this woman mess with your head, Frank," a woman's voice said.

"That's not what's happening, Captain," Jakes said.

Interesting, I thought. Jakes's boss was a woman.

"It's not? Then you tell me what's happenin', Detective."

"She's a resource," Jakes argued. "She knows the soap world inside out."

"So you're telling me this whole case is connected to the soaps?"

"Well . . . yeah." Jakes sounded like he was speaking to a child.

I heard the rustle of papers and then the woman said, "Did you know that one of those five cases was closed? Someone was arrested!"

"I know," he said. "Len told me."

"We heard from the Canadian police that they arrested someone, Frank! He confessed."

"That may be so," Jakes said. "But the other four are still open."

"You've got four cases here that I'm not convinced are connected. Look, Frank, work your four cases, but I don't want to hear the phrase 'serial killer.' And I sure as hell don't want to see it in the papers."

"Laura—"

"Captain to you, Detective."

"Okay, Captain—"

"And I don't want you talking to that soap diva," the captain said.

"She's not a diva!" Jakes said sharply, defending me. That really made me smile. "Look, Captain, she's got inside knowledge—"

"I'm not convinced all these men were killed because they were on soap operas, Frank. That means I'm not convinced she can be helpful. But I do know she can be a distraction. And she'll attract the paparazzi."

"They were either on a soap or auditioned for one," he corrected. "And she's my . . . my link to that world."

"Listen to yourself," the captain scoffed. "You sound like a narc talkin' about his connection. Or worse, a junkie. Get out of my office, Detective," the captain said. "You're wastin' my time."

Suddenly the door swung opened. I caught a glimpse of an attractive, middle-aged woman in a suit behind a desk before Jakes came out and slammed the door behind him. He saw me and stopped.

"Alex."

"I, uh, your partner told me to sit here and wait," I said lamely.

"Did you hea—" he started, pointing at the door. "What am I saying? Of course you heard everything."

"Not everything."

"But enough," he said. "Okay, come on. Let's get out of here before the boss sees you."

I stood and hurried after him. "You never told me your boss was a woman."

"It never came up," he said. As we passed his partner's desk, he said, "We're going out for a drink. You want to come with us, Len?"

"Sure." He grabbed his sports coat from the back of his chair.

We all went out the door, into the hall and down to the elevator.

"So that's what you call not causing you any trouble?" I asked in the elevator.

Chapter 31

The three of us stopped at a nearby coffee shop. Davis had a latte, Jakes an iced tea and I had a turkey and Swiss on a baguette with onion rings as a chaser. I was starving.

"We need to clear the air," Jakes said.

Davis and I stared at each other.

Jakes continued. "Len, any trouble I'm in—or I get into—is not going to impact you."

"I'm your partner, Frank."

"Neither one of us picked this partnership, Len. You want to walk away, that's fine with me."

"That what you want?"

"Actually, no," Jakes said. "I prefer the devil I know, if you catch my drift."

"I do."

I did, too. Maybe they weren't a perfect match, but at least they knew each other, and Jakes had no way of knowing who he might end up with if they broke their partnership off now.

"So we stay partners?" Jakes asked.

"Yes."

"And I want to keep using Alex as a resource. Is that okay?"

"Is it okay with the captain?"

"No."

"Then why do it?"

"Because these are my cases and I call the shots," Jakes said.

"And what will the captain say when she finds out you kept working with Alex?"

"When we solve these murders," Jakes replied, "she won't care."

"Maybe not."

"Len," Jakes said, "I think it would be better for you if you weren't around Alex."

"Actually," Davis said, pushing back his chair, "that's fine with me." He gave me a dirty look and stood up.

"Oh, and Len?"

"Yes?"

"She didn't leave *The Yearning Tide* to hurt you," Jakes said, "so get over yourself."

Davis gave Jakes a look, appeared ready to say something and then shook his head and left.

Jakes turned to look. "Okay, now you."

"Wait a minute," I said. "I heard what went on in your boss's office. How can you say you're not in trouble because of me?"

"Because I'm not," he said. "Look, Alex, I never blame my problems on other people. If I did I'd be pointing the finger at Len a lot more."

"Come on, Jakes," I said. "If you're just going to lie to me—"

"Okay, wait," he said, holding up his hands. "If I

tell you what's going on with my boss, you have to promise not to laugh."

"I won't."

"And you might not believe me."

"I will," I said. "I promise. Just don't lie."

"Okay," he said, looking uncomfortable. "My boss is Captain Laura Carpenter. A woman."

"I got that much."

"Well . . . she has the hots for me."

I didn't laugh. I wanted to, because he looked so miserable, but I held it in.

"What makes you think she has the hots for you?"

"She kind of told me."

"Kind of told you? Or you think she told you? Because I've known men who can't tell the difference."

"Believe me," he said, "when a woman makes a move and asks me to go home with her, I notice."

"She did that?"

"Yes," he said. "She did it once. I turned her down. Since then she hasn't tried again, but she's been . . ." He groped for a good phrase.

"Making your life miserable?"

"Yes."

"Has she tried it with anyone else?"

"Not that I know of," he said.

"Did you tell anyone? Your partner?"

"No," he said. "I told you. Len and I aren't that close."

"So he has no idea why she's riding you."

"No."

"You know," I said, "I got a glimpse of her. She seems . . . attractive."

"She's okay," he said. "A few years older than me, but not bad."

"Then what's the problem? You're single, right?"

He rolled his eyes. "She's not my type. And . . . I guess Len told her I had asked you out after that whole Marcy Blanchard case. Ever since she's been kind of . . . snarky."

"So, wait . . . Is she pissed off at me?"

"I'd say yes," he said, "which is probably why she doesn't want you around."

"And what happens if she tried to make *my* life miserable?"

"Don't worry," he said. "I won't let that happen."

"But you still want me in on this investigation?"

"Definitely."

"Why?" I asked. "As far as I can see, I didn't add much to it yesterday."

"Well," he said, "that's what I wanted to discuss with you." He grabbed an onion ring from my plate. "Let's talk."

Chapter 32

"Okay," I said, "but I need a dessert." When we both had a piece of cake in front of us, I asked, "What about one of the murders being solved?"

"Kyle Hansen was murdered in Canada, and apparently they've made an arrest and closed the case."

"What if he's the wrong man?"

"They have a confession."

"What if they—you know—coerced it out of him? I mean, it happens all the time."

"Sometimes, sure," he said. "I can check into it a little further, but I think we should concentrate on the other four."

Before I could say anything, my cell sang out. I looked at the caller ID and saw it was Connie. She had left a couple of messages I hadn't even bothered to listen to. Guilt set in so I decided to hear what she had to say.

"Sorry, Jakes. I really need to take this." He shrugged and I got up and moved away from the table. "How've you been, Connie?"

"Doll, I've been good. I miss you, though. Are you feeling better?"

"I am. Thanks. And I'm sorry if I hurt your feelings. I just needed to step away."

"I get it, Al. This business can be such a bitch! Now, I got a request. . . ." Before I could object, she went on. "Hold your horses! You're gonna love it." I let her tell me and she was right.

The Academy of Television was known for hosting a series of "An Evening with . . ." programs. You know: "An Evening with the Cast of *ER*," "the Writers of *30 Rock*," et cetera. Apparently they were doing "An Evening with the Leading Ladies of Daytime" and wanted my participation. It would be me along with Susan Lucci, Melody Thomas Scott and Kim Zimmer. I was very flattered and excited about the idea of speaking about what I know and love at a forum of this magnitude.

"You're right, Connie. I do love it. Count me in. When is it?"

"It's on next Monday night. Seven to ten p.m. They're happy to send a car. They'll be over the moon to know you're going to be a part of it. Thanks, doll. I'll fill you in with more details as we get closer. Now, there's one more thing. It's a new game show that puts celebrities in clown suits and asks them—"

"Connie! Don't push your luck. I love ya. Gotta go." I pushed "end" and walked back over to Jakes.

"Everything okay?" he asked.

"Yeah, just some business. Where were we? I think you were about to tell me about the fifth one." I sat down.

"Mason Stone," Jakes said. "He lived here but was

from San Francisco. That's something Len's been trying to do, get in touch with his family up there."

"So they don't even know that he's dead yet?"

"No."

"That's terrible."

"We'll notify them as soon as we can," Jakes said,
"because we also want to question them."

"We," I said. "When you say we . . ."

"I'm including you, Alex."

"Okay, let's get back to that," I said. "Like I said, I
didn't add a thing yesterday—"

"Alex, just because you haven't contributed yet
doesn't mean you won't."

"You sure you're not using me to piss off your
boss?"

"Believe me," he said, "I don't have to try to piss
her off . . . but am I waving you under her nose? No
way. I consider you a valuable resource."

"Why?"

"Because soap operas—and women—seem to
be the two things all these cases have in common.
Granted, Jackson was the only one working regu-
larly, but the others have auditioned and, for all we
know, could've played some bit parts."

"I'm still waiting to hear what my contribution is
going to be."

"Okay, Len's trying to find the Stone family," he
explained. "I have to follow up on all the interviews
I did yesterday. It catches people off guard when you
come right back at them."

"And me?"

He took out his notebook, tore a slip of paper from
it, put it on the table and pushed it toward me. It had
the names of four soap operas on it.

"Do you know people at those shows?"

"I know someone at almost every show," I told him. "It's the nature of the business—especially if they're on the same network."

"Good," he said. "I want you to get in there and find out what you can about our dead guys. Who auditioned for what part, and who got the job."

"I can do that," I said. "How do you know which shows they auditioned for?"

"Agents," he said. "That was the one thing we were able to find in all their apartments: the names and addresses of their agents."

I picked up the slip of paper. "Good. Now I'll feel useful."

He called the waitress over and took care of the bill. We had all driven there in our own cars, so as we left the place he took my arm and walked me to mine.

"I'll give you a call to see if you found anything out," he said. "Remember, we're on the clock."

"If I get anything, I'll call you first," I promised.

He waited while I unlocked my door. I opened it and then turned and leaned on it.

"You could ask these questions, Jakes," I said, "or have another cop do it. Why me?"

"Jesus, Alex," he said, "could we put this question to bed?"

"Humor me."

"Okay," he said. "People lie to the police. It's automatic."

"But if they didn't do anything—"

"Everybody feels guilty about something," he said. "It's a reflex. Believe me, you have a better chance of being told the truth than I do."

I thought a moment and then shrugged and said, "Okay, I accept that."

"Good. Talk to you soon."

As I pulled away from the curb, I could see him in the rearview mirror, watching.

Chapter 33

When I got home and flipped on the lights, Sarah scared the you-know-what out of me by yelling, "Surprise! Mommeeeeee," and running into my arms. I got over my fright quickly, squeezed the stuffing out of her and covered her with tickle kisses. I was hugging her again when my mom came walking in.

"Hi, Mom," I said, looking at her over Sarah's head.

"Hi, honey!"

I released Sarah long enough to give my mom a kiss and a big hug.

"I'm so glad you're both home," I told her. "Why didn't you call me? I would've come and picked you up at the airport."

"Sarah said she wanted to surprise you. It was just a short cab ride."

I turned and caught Sarah as she jumped into my arms again.

"I missed you so much, Mommy," she said. "I didn't like the Middlewest so much."

"Oh, honey, there are good things about it and not so good things. Just like here."

"I like living here the best," she said. "This is where my room is."

Perfect little girl logic.

"I made dinner," Mom said. "Hope you're hungry."

"I would've taken you both out."

"Nonsense," she said, turning and heading back to the kitchen. "I'll have it on the table in no time."

I played with Sarah for a few more minutes and then listened during dinner while she told all of her "Middlewest" adventures. After that we watched some TV together while Mom did the dishes and cleaned the kitchen. I felt guilty leaving the cleanup to her, but Sarah would not let me go. By the time I read her a bedtime story and tucked her in, my mother had two cups of tea ready.

We sat on the sofa together with our tea. Things felt more normal than they had in weeks.

"Now tell me what's been going on, dear," Mom said, "and don't leave anything out."

My mother was quiet by the time I finished telling her everything—well, almost everything.

"Mom?"

"Alex," she said finally, "I understand what happened at the Emmy Awards was traumatic, and you'd like to help find who killed that young man, Jackson, but you have to remember you have Sarah waiting for you at home."

"Well," I said, "up to now she's been away with you, but now that's she's back I have every intention—"

"No," she said, putting her hand on my knee. "I mean all the time, not just now. You got hurt the last time, remember? You could have gotten killed. And then where would Sarah be without a mother? For all intents and purposes, Sarah has already lost her father. And where would I be without my daughter?"

I put my hand over hers. Little did she know Randy was back in the picture. Or trying to be, anyway.

"I understand, Mom," I said, "but this is different. I'm not in danger, and I won't be."

"You know that for sure?"

I took my hand away from hers. "Well, of course I know that, Mom."

She patted my knee and said, "Just checking, dear." She stood up, picked up both cups, but didn't leave the room. "What about Paul?"

"What about him?" I asked, not meeting her eyes. "He's still away, working."

"I assumed that," she said. "I meant . . . what about you and him?"

"What are you asking me?"

"I'm not too old to recognize attraction to the opposite sex, Alex," she said. "I saw it last time between you and that detective. I assume it's still there."

"Mom—"

"I'm just saying, you almost lost Paul last time," she said. "Do you want to risk it this time?"

"Mom . . . I haven't done anything. . . ."

"I believe you—I do. You haven't done anything . . . yet. I'm just . . . being a mother, you know?"

"Yes," I said, "I know."

As she left the room and went back to the kitchen, I understood what she was saying. After all, I was a mother, too, and wanted what was best for Sarah. I didn't ever want her to get hurt . . . not even a little.

My mother didn't want me to get hurt. A skinned knee, a bruised ego, a broken heart . . . they all hurt.

Mom came back into the room to give me a hug and a kiss on the cheek. "Good night, Alex."

"Night, Mom. I'm really glad you're back."

"That's nice to hear," she said. "So am I.

"Maybe we can all go to the beach and have a picnic tomorrow."

"All right, Mom," I said. "That sounds like fun!"

As I passed by the window on my way to bed, I noticed a car parked across the street. The cop nodded to me and gave me a thumbs-up. Jakes hadn't missed a beat. He already had someone watching Sarah. I would sleep well tonight. My family was home and safe!

Chapter 34

I went to the studio Monday prepared to do Detective Jakes's bidding. One of the shows he wanted me to check out, *Too Late for Yesterday*, taped in the same building we did, so it was a simple thing to walk over there before I started work.

I had spent the entire weekend with Sarah and my mom. I knew I'd missed my little girl, but even I didn't know how much until I got to have breakfast with her Saturday morning. She chattered away about her trip and had a lot to tell me for someone who claimed she didn't like it. When she asked me what we were going to do that day, I told her that Saturday and Sunday were for her. We'd do whatever she wanted to do. After that I might have her and my mom go stay with George and Wayne for a few days while the whole Randy thing got sorted out. I was probably being overprotective. So what?

"Hey, Alex," Danielle Asbury said as I walked into her office. "What brings you over to the competition?"

She was kidding, of course. Our shows were on the same network, but the last I heard *The Bare and Brazen* was a little higher in the ratings. Unfortunately, we were both trailing *The Yearning Tide*, which—despite my departure—was highly rated.

Danielle was the associate producer on her show. Associate producers do a little bit of everything and a whole lot of other things, including knowing the ins and outs of their respective shows.

"I have a question about an actor named Aaron Summers, Danielle."

Danielle frowned. "I don't think we've ever had an Aaron Summers on the show. At least, not during my tenure." Danielle was in her fifties, and her tenure probably went back twenty years.

"No, you haven't," I said, "but you did have someone by that name audition for a part that he didn't get. I'd like to know when and for what part."

"What's this about, Alex?"

"Aaron Summers is dead," I said. "He was killed in a way similar to Jackson Masters. He was also the same general type."

"Are you playing detective, Alex?"

"I'm . . . just helping the police with their inquiries."

"Because we might ask them for a warrant for this information," she asked with a smile, "but we'll give it to you freely?"

I seriously doubted the police would need a warrant. The information wasn't protected or anything, but I said, "Something like that."

"Well . . . I saw what happened to you at the Emmys, you poor thing. Let me see what I can find out."

"Great," I said, and gave her my cell number.

* * *

After hair and makeup I still had some time before going on the set. I decided to call Danielle's counterpart on one of the other shows, *The Tears of Tomorrow*. I asked for the person I thought had the job and discovered that she had left several months ago.

"She had a baby," the man on the other end of the phone said.

"Wow, good for her," I said. "So, who replaced her?"

"I did," he said. "My name's Eddie."

"Eddie, this is Alex Peterson," I said. "I'm—"

"I know who you are, Ms. Peterson! How can I help you?"

I gave him the same spiel I'd given Danielle, adding that I was "helping the police with their inquiries," before he asked any questions.

"Sure," he said, "I'd be glad to help. Give me your number and I'll call you when I find something out. And what were those names again?"

I gave him all the names.

"Got it. I'll give you a call."

"Thanks, Eddie."

"You're welcome."

I broke the connection just as they called me on the set.

To get information I needed from the other shows, I could call or drive over to their studios and talk to the right people. In my dressing room I decided to do both—first call and then drive over. Unfortunately, I got the same word from both shows. The person I needed would not be in until the next day. If Jakes called me later in the evening—and I fully expected him to—he'd have to be satisfied that I'd made inquiries at two of the four shows and was waiting for the replies.

I didn't notice until I was in my car that there was a message on my cell that had come in while I was on the set.

"Voicemail!" I shouted for my Bluetooth to hear. Nothing. *"Voicemail!"* I yelled again. Two more times and it finally connected. I pushed in my code.

The message was from Danielle over at *Too Late for Yesterday.* She said she had the info I wanted and suggested I call her right back, because she had the next two days off.

"Hey, Danielle."

"Hey, Alex. I've got that information for you, girl," Danielle said. "Aaron Summers auditioned for the role of Cole Weathers early last year. He didn't get it, but he came close."

"Who did get it, Danielle?"

"Jed Foreman."

I knew that name. He had been on the show for a few months now.

"And he was the first choice? He didn't get it because Aaron Summers . . . died?"

"Oh, God, no," she said. "Jed was our first choice as soon as he walked in the door."

"So when you say Aaron was close . . ."

"If Jed wasn't able to take the job for some reason, we would've called Aaron. Does this help?"

I was damned if I knew. I'd found out that Aaron Summers had auditioned for both my old show and *Too Late for Yesterday. Did* that help? That was up to Jakes to say, but I told her it did and thanked her for the information. I closed my phone and started the engine. I was deep in thought as I pulled out the gate, waving absently at the guard in his little house.

I found out later that if I'd been more aware of my surroundings I could have saved myself a lot of grief.

Chapter 35

I had dinner with Sarah and Mom.

My mother had been cooking since she got home. I realized how much I'd missed that. I had been eating out often or just preparing something small for myself.

"I think I've gained weight just in the few days you've been home, Mom."

"That's okay, honey," she said. "As usual, you're too thin. You could use a few extra pounds."

"Thanks. Tell that to the camera. What's a couple of pounds, right?"

I had just tucked Sarah into bed when the phone rang. My mother answered it and then held it out to me.

"It's your police detective."

"He's not my—" I started to say, but dropped it. Instead I just took the cordless phone from her.

"Hi," he said. "I see your family's home."

"Yes, they got back a couple of days ago."

"That's nice," he said. "Did you, um, were you able to find out anything for me?"

I told him how the day had gone: that I talked to associate producers from two shows, but not the other two. I told him what Danielle had confided about Aaron Summers. While I was talking, I walked to the front window and looked out. There was a big 4x4 truck parked at the curb. Paparazzi? One of Jakes's guys? I didn't think so and watched it pull away.

"I'll try to get some more tomorrow," I said. "Anything on your end?"

"Nothing new or meaningful," he said. "I'll, uh, talk to you again tomorrow night, if that's okay?"

He sounded like a man with something on his mind, something he didn't want to talk about. He hadn't mentioned finding out anything about Randy, and I hadn't asked. That wouldn't make the problem go away, though.

"That's fine, Jakes," I said. "Talk to you tomorrow."

He hung up.

Tuesday was much like Monday, except for the fact that I ended up having to work late. There had been some kind of a malfunction with the videotape machines, and all the scenes that had been taped that morning had been erased! We ended up having to retape fifteen scenes and still finish the rest of the show.

I was beat, and why wouldn't I be? When taping finally ended, it was a little after one a.m. As I was heading down the stairs toward the parking lot, I ran into one of our cameramen. He was a great guy I'd known forever. We'd worked on different shows together and went way back. Shel—I assume that was short for Sheldon—had recently married a woman with two children. We chatted as we walked, and he told me the whole way how he adored both of them—especially the little girl, who was six.

"But that's not right, is it, Alex?" he asked. "Favoring one child over the other?"

"It doesn't sound like you're favoring anyone, Shel. And besides, it's that daughter-dad thing. Even though you're a stepdad, it still applies, don't ya think?"

He was quiet for a few seconds as a slight smile crept over his face. "Yeah, that's right. I am a dad now. I guess it does apply. Thanks for pointing that out." He hugged me good night. "See you tomorrow."

Dads and daughters. What trauma was my own daughter suffering because of her father not being in the picture? Maybe I had to let bygones be bygones with Randy. Even though I couldn't stand the thought of sharing custody. Maybe I had to. For my daughter's sake.

I pulled out of my spot and drove around to the guard's post. There were more cars than you'd think still in the lot at that time of night. The guard stuck his head out, took a look at me and then waved as I left—deep in thought again.

I'd heard from Eddie over at *The Tears of Tomorrow* hours ago. I had found a message on my cell during a break so I called him about Mason Stone and the part he'd auditioned for but didn't get.

"Not even close," Eddie said when I got him on the phone. "Looked the part, but he just wasn't good enough. At least, that's what somebody wrote here."

I was going to ask how Mason had taken it, but Eddie wouldn't have known.

"Thank you so much, Eddie."

"Sure, Alexis. Anything else I can do to help, just let me know."

I had managed to get hold of someone at the other two shows—*The Best Days Are Ahead* and *The Depths of the Sea*. They were looking for the information I needed and hopefully would get back to me tomorrow.

There were three other messages left on my phone between nine p.m. and one a.m. One was from Sarah, saying good night and she loved me.

The second message was from Jakes, wanting to know if I had any information for him.

The third message was from Randy. My stomach did a flip when I heard his voice. "Hey, babe. Heard your mom and Sarah are back home. Time for me to see my little girl again—and don't think you can stop me."

Damn it, what was he planning? I hadn't planned to answer the other messages. It was just too late. But the message from Randy made me rethink calling Jakes back.

I jumped on the 10 and headed home. As is always the case when you're driving late and there are only a few cars on the road, one idiot gets right behind you with their bright lights on. And even if it's not their brights, they're blinding. I especially hate the blu-ish lights people are getting now—and SUVs are the worst. I should talk—I do have my kid car—but still! They're so high you can't escape them. They come at you from your rearview mirror like laser beams.

There was a truck behind me with the pain in the ass lights, and I was just thinking how they were worse than SUVs when it closed on me fast and bumped me. The impact made my head jerk back, and as I fought the wheel we went hurtling past my exit. I turned my head to look. He had dropped back but was still there. It was obvious he'd hit me on purpose, but why? I started looking for a place to get off and turn back when he suddenly appeared in my rearview mirror and hit me a second time. My head jerked again, and in order to try to get away from him I had no choice but to drive onto PCH.

Even in LA at that time of night, the Pacific Coast Highway was almost empty. There I was with the truck chasing me, feeling so alone. And he *was* chasing me. Of this there was no doubt. I pressed hard on the accelerator, wishing now that I'd been driving my beautiful, powerful Porsche instead of my kid car, the Ford Explorer.

It was a joke thinking I might be able to outrun him. I didn't know if he was trying to scare me or hurt me but, I realized it was time to get help. I yelled at my Bluetooth, "911!" Nothing. "911! 911! SHIT!" Still nothing. "911! 911!"

My cell phone had fallen down to the floorboard. I reached to grab it just as the truck came up behind me and rammed me again. This time it was so hard that my head jerked and I screamed. The impact sounded impossibly loud to me. I tried to catch a look at the driver. That's hard enough using a rearview mirror, but the truck also had dark tinted windows.

I switched lanes, weaving back and forth as I tried to avoid being rammed again. I knew if he hit me any harder, I might lose control of the Ford.

As I looked in the rearview mirror and watched the road ahead of me, hoping to see a police car, I couldn't stop thinking about my little girl at home in bed. What if she woke up in the morning and found out her mother was gone? "Please, God. Please. No!"

There were few headlights coming southbound on PCH. The truck could have tried to ram me into an oncoming car, but for a while he seemed content to just follow me. Then, when he started to catch up again and I realized where we were, I knew what he wanted to do.

We were at a deadly section of PCH where there were no houses or guardrails, and a treacherous cliff was only a few southbound lanes over. A plunge over the side would be fatal.

No sooner had I thought it than I saw the headlights coming up behind me fast.

I braced for the impact even as I swerved to avoid it.

Chapter 36

. . . slow motion . . .
  . . . no, stop-action . . .
  . . . flashing lights . . .
  . . . actual lights? . . .
  . . . or was it . . . my eyes? . . .
  . . . I felt the impact from behind . . .
  . . . then again from the side . . .
  . . . hit my head this time . . .
  . . . I fought the wheel, but then I was skidding . . .
  . . . sideways . . .
  . . . across the highway . . .
  . . . oh, God, if there was any oncoming traffic . . .
  . . . what was it? Steer into the skid . . . that was
it . . . or risk flipping over . . .
  . . . sirens . . .
  . . . lights . . .
  . . . spinning . . .
  . . . spinning or dizzy? . . .
  . . . around and around . . .
  . . . heading for the edge . . .
  . . . screeching metal . . .
  . . . sparks . . .

. . . somebody screaming . . .
. . . grabbing for the door . . .
. . . screaming . . .
. . . somebody . . .
. . . me?

Chapter 37

"Alex?"

I heard the screeching of metal, the car door protesting as it opened.

"Alex? Can you hear me?"

I felt something wet on my head, which hurt like hell. I reached up to touch it.

"Open your eyes, Alex. Look at me!"

The voice was loud, commanding me. I didn't want to open my eyes, but I did.

"Jakes?"

"Thank God," he said. His face was illuminated by the light from inside the car. He looked worried.

"I'm not dead?"

"No," Jakes said, "you're not dead—but not by much."

"Sir?" someone said from behind him. "Can we get to her?"

"Alex, I'm going to let the EMT have a look at you, all right?"

"Sure . . . Um, my head hurts. . . ."

"He'll have a look," Jakes promised. He withdrew and a young man took his place. He asked me some questions—my name, what day it was, things like that—shined a light in my eyes, told me to follow his finger. Weirdly, I noticed he needed a manicure.

"How—Where am I?" I asked.

"You're in your car."

"I know that," I said, "but I seem to remember I was . . . heading for the edge. I was going to jump out, but . . . I think I hit my head."

"You did," he said. "I'm going to take care of that now."

"But . . . how did I not go over the edge?"

"You'll have to ask the detective about that," the EMT said. "It looks like he saved your life."

"H-how?"

"Well, I don't know all the facts, but it appears he used his own car to keep you from being rammed and pushed over the edge."

"B-but how?"

"Again," he said, "you'll have to ask the detective. Now hold still, ma'am, and I'll take care of this cut."

When the EMT was done, Jakes appeared in the doorway again and asked, "Do you want to try standing up?"

"Yes, thanks," I said.

He extended his hands and I took them. He pulled me to my feet. I either fell against him or he pulled me to him for a brief hug, but I was on my feet again so quickly I couldn't be sure.

"What happened?" I asked. I turned and looked at the car. I couldn't see much, it was so dark. The air felt good on my face, though. In fact, it felt good to be alive.

"You were hit repeatedly in the back," he said. "Then on the passenger side. I was coming from the other direction when you went careening across the southbound lanes, heading for the edge."

"B-but . . . I didn't go over."

"No," Jakes said. "Both passenger side tires blew out. The metal rims scraping along the ground slowed you down enough to keep you from going over."

"Then what?" I wanted him to get to the part where he saved my life.

"Well, it looked like the truck was going to ram you over the edge."

"And?"

"Well . . ." He seemed uncomfortable. "I pulled my car up alongside yours."

"You got between me and the truck?"

"Yes."

"Your car is no match for a large truck. He might have pushed both of us over the edge," I said.

"He might have," Jake said, "but instead he just took off."

"You saved me," I said simply.

"But I didn't keep you from getting hurt. I'm so sorry."

I couldn't stop staring at him. Something wasn't making any sense. "What were you doing here? How did you know I needed help?"

"And I didn't get the license plate of the truck," he went on.

"Jakes . . . answer me."

"Well, in this case it was just luck. But after you told me about Randy, I've . . . been keeping an eye on you. Just in case. I didn't like the way it sounded, so . . ."

"Do you think that was Randy in the truck?" It

would be hard for me to believe Randy could be a killer but stranger things have happened.

"I'm not a hundred percent sure. I have some people keeping an eye out and they haven't seen him, but maybe he slipped by."

"Frank . . ." I reached out for his face and gently held it in my hands. "Thank you."

"Well. That is my job, you—"

I stopped his words by putting my lips over his and kissing him. We came together like two long-lost lovers who had been separated by some tragedy. I looked deeply into his eyes and felt something that I was pretty certain I'd never felt before. He seemed to be feeling it, too. It was amazing. And all-encompassing. And I didn't want it to ever end.

Just then the young EMT walked up and cleared his throat.

"Uh, sorry to, um, interrupt, ma'am, but we have to take you to the hospital," he sort of muttered, looking at us sideways. Jakes and I quickly disengaged but kept staring at each other like we were seeing each other for the first time.

"I don't have to go, do I?"

"Oh, yes," Jakes interjected. "You do. The ambulance will take you, and I'll meet you there."

"My car—"

"We'll get it towed," he said. "Don't worry. It'll be safe." His hand brushed my hair from my cheek. He spoke softly like we were the only ones there. "You have to, Alex. We need to make sure you're absolutely okay." He gave me a look like his life depended on my well-being, and I thought I was going to melt right there in the middle of Pacific Coast Highway.

The EMT led me to the ambulance as Jakes walked

to his car. We were both looking over our shoulders at each other, still not willing to let the moment end.

What the hell was going on? Whatever it was, I knew I wanted more of it.

Chapter 38

No concussion, but three stitches. A true professional, I was already wondering how we could work the stitches into the storyline.

Jakes was in the waiting room when I came out.

"Doesn't look too bad," he said.

I touched the bandage over my eye. "The doctor said it will look worse in the morning," I said.

"With a little luck you won't have a black eye," Jakes said. "That looks high enough."

"You didn't have to wait," I said, although I was so very glad he did. "I can call George or my mother."

"Your mother has Sarah," he said. "I'm already here. Come on; I'll take you home."

We walked out the emergency room exit to his car. He was very solicitous, offering to bring the car to me, but I told him I could walk—even though my legs felt like wet noodles. I wasn't sure if that was because of the stitches or because of what had happened with Jakes. Maybe both.

He held the passenger door open for me and then got in behind the wheel.

We were looking at each other shyly, both with silly

grins. Neither one of us seemed to know what to say until finally I managed to ask, "What about my car?"

"It's been towed," Jakes said. "I'll help you get it back when you're ready."

We rode in silence for several minutes and then he became all cop. "Did you see the driver?"

"No," I said, "the windows were tinted."

"Did you get the license plate?"

"I tried to get a look when he, I assume it was a he, was following me. There were no plates, at least not in front."

"Had you ever seen the vehicle before?" he asked. "Following you, maybe?"

"Not that I noticed," I said. "But . . ."

"But what?"

"I did notice a truck outside my house when I was on the phone with you the other night. For a second I thought it might be paparazzi. I didn't think much of it."

"Same one?"

"I . . . I can't say."

"Same color?"

"I think so."

"Didn't see a driver?"

"No, but it doesn't feel like something Randy would do. He's capable of a lot of things—but murder? I don't think so."

"I tend to agree with you. This has to do with the actor murders. Someone is pissed."

Silence settled over us again. Then he said, "You know, you should probably stay out of this from now on."

"Yes," I said, "I probably should."

"But you won't, will you?"

I looked at him. He was staring straight ahead.

"I'm going to give it some serious consideration," I said.

He pulled up in front of my house and turned off the engine. He was looking out his window, thinking about something. Then he turned to me and held my hands.

"Look, I don't know what this is between us. I do know it's pretty amazing." I was about to jump in when he said, "Let me finish. I care too much about you to lose you. So if you stay involved in this case, I'll be stuck on you like glue." He held my eyes. "You got a problem with that?"

I absolutely did not have a problem with that. Jakes being stuck on me in any way, shape or form only felt like a good thing. To all different parts of my body.

"I can't say I do," I answered.

Suddenly he grabbed me and kissed me so hard it took my breath away. After a long moment he pulled away and whispered, "You want me to walk you in?" His lips were still touching mine.

"No," I stammered. "I'll, um, be fine. I—I have enough to explain to Sarah and my mother."

Still with our lips slightly touching, he added, "And I think you have something to explain to Paul, don't you?" We were looking into each other's eyes.

"I do. Yes, I do." I took a deep breath and we kissed again.

When we pulled apart, he said, "So, about tonight— the truck, you getting hit—we agree it was deliberate, right?"

"No doubt about it. That shithead followed me from the studio and must have planned the whole thing," I said. Just thinking about it was pissing me off.

"Uh-oh. This is bad."

"Yeah, it's bad. Some asshole tried to run me off the road."

"No, this. You're gettin' mad."

"So what?" I asked. "Shouldn't I be mad?"

"Your life probably flashed in front of your eyes as you were skidding across the highway," he said. "And you probably thought about Sarah."

"I did." I blinked at him. "What's your point?"

"And you might have even said a prayer. 'God, get me out of this, let me see my baby again, and I promise I'll forget all about this business and leave it to the police.' "

"Jakes—"

"But now you're gettin' angry, and by tomorrow you'll be livid, and you'll forget all about your promise to God or to yourself."

"I'll be careful. And you're going to be stuck on me, right? Like glue?" I even liked the thought of it.

He turned back so that he was facing front again.

I reached out and touched his arm. "I really will be careful. I want a chance to find out what this is with us as much as you do. And you know how I feel about my daughter. I won't do anything stupid, I promise."

"You better not." He gave me another kiss.

"I'd better go inside now or I won't go at all."

I opened the door, started to get out.

"Alex!"

"Yes?" I looked at him over my shoulder.

"I'm glad I was there for you. When you needed me."

I took a moment to really see him. "So am I."

Chapter 39

Jakes was right. I woke up pissed.

After he'd left I had to convince my mother I was all right, that the hospital had released me, not seeing fit to give me a bed for the night. Thank God I didn't have to see Sarah—or, more to the point, Sarah didn't have to see me—right away.

When I woke I went into the bathroom to look at myself. What I saw made my mood worse. I was angry as hell at whoever had been in that truck. Neither Jakes nor I had asked the obvious question last night—why me? It was obviously because I was nosing around in these murders. The question I had was, why me and not Jakes? He was the danger. He was a detective, for Pete's sake.

Jakes had been right about the black eye not showing up. But my head was sore. I took the bandage off to see how it looked. Three stitches is really nothing, not in the scheme of things. Fifty stitches—now that would have been something.

I put a fresh Band-Aid on the eye—the small cut bisected my eyebrow. I'd worry about that later. Maybe I'd have to switch my career path and start being a character actress. They found more interesting roles to play, anyway.

"She didn't notice," I said to my mom after breakfast, as Sarah went to her room to put on her little wet suit for surf camp.

"Good," my mother said. "I'm glad." Her tone was clipped and cold. She was still upset with me—not because I'd gotten hurt, but because of how and why I'd been involved. I didn't blame her, but I was still too mad to just walk away.

While I got dressed for the day, I figured all I had to do was stay alert from now on, watch for a dark truck and continue to try to get the soap information that Jakes wanted. I still had two shows to work on.

Sarah and I left, my mother's disapproving glare following me to the garage. I could feel it burning a hole between my shoulder blades. I pulled my Porsche, Marilyn, out of the garage and let Sarah in, and then closed the garage door. I pulled out onto the road and looked in my rearview mirror to make sure Sarah's police shadow was right behind me. There was no way my little girl was going anywhere without someone watching her every move.

Sarah chattered the whole way. When we got to surf camp she kissed me good-bye, grabbed her lunch and started to step out of the car. Suddenly she turned, looked at me and asked, "What happened to your eye?"

"I bumped it, sweetie," I said. Which was the truth.

"Does it hurt?"

"Not very much."

"Is that why we're using Marilyn?"

"Yes, honey, that's why."

"Don't bump it anymore, Mommy."

"I won't, sweetie. I love you. Don't forget your towel. And eat the carrots I put in your lunch." I grabbed her Hawaiian print towel and gave it to her.

"I love you, too, Mommeeeee," she said as she skipped away, looking every bit like a little black seal in her wet suit. The car that had followed us to the beach pulled up along side me.

"Hi, ma'am! I'm Officer Kavanaugh. A friend of Frank's. I just wanted to introduce myself." This impossibly strong, muscular, not to mention good-looking cop was my daughter's protector? How nice.

"I appreciate that, Officer. You make sure Sarah is safe, okay? Are you going in the water, too?" I laughed.

"I hadn't planned on it. But if it's necessary . . ." And he held up a pair of brightly colored swim trunks.

"Wow. You come prepared! I'm impressed." I chuckled. And then more seriously, "Thank you for what you're doing. I truly appreciate it."

"It's my pleasure, ma'am. Actually I should thank you. I owe Frank a lot. It's nice to be able to do something for him for a change. He's a good guy." He looked in the direction of the water, "Uh-oh! They're getting ready to go out. I gotta go! You take care!" And he drove off to park.

He wasn't kidding. Frank Jakes was a good guy. The more I learned about Jakes, the more I was sure of it. They don't come any better.

When I got to work I had to talk to the producer, Sean Peters, about my eye.

"You can't tape your scenes that way, Alex," he said. "Any suggestions?"

"Not a problem. I talked to the hairdresser and I'll just cut some bangs. That should cover everything." The show must go on and all that, after all.

"I appreciate that, Alex. You're a professional. The last thing we need are any delays. Budget issues, you know?" he said.

I knew all about the budget issues. It seems that every soap opera is plagued with them these days.

"Happy to help." I ran off, changed my clothes and cut some bangs. I taped my two scenes and was out the door in an hour and a half.

I called the associate producer of *The Depths of the Sea* again and got his voice mail. I got through to the associate producer of *The Best Days Are Ahead* right away.

"Come on over here, Alex," Tilda James said. "I'll have the information by the time you get here, and then we can have lunch."

Lunch? Well, why not? You can always make new friends, right?

"Okay, Tilda," I said. "I'll be over there in a half hour."

"Great," she said. "I'm a big fan. I've always wanted to meet you."

Wasn't that nice? You never know when you might need another show to fall back on. It sure came in handy after *The Tide* dried up for me.

Chapter 40

The Depths of the Sea and *The Best Days Are Ahead* were both taped over at the UBM studios in Silver Lake, about a fifteen-minute drive from my studio. I drove up to the gate and gave the guard my name, and they let me right in. It's always fun to go to another studio and see how they do things. It kind of feels like new possibilities. I found my way up to the production offices of *The Best Days Are Ahead*. They had large black-and-white photos of their cast members on the walls. A lot of them I knew; some I didn't.

The receptionist walked in. "May I help you?" When I turned around she said, "Oh, hi! You're here to see Tilda, right? She's expecting you. One second!" And she exited down the hall.

Tilda turned out to be younger than I had thought over the phone, probably in her late twenties. And, as she had promised, was a big fan of mine. She was actually kind of gushing as we walked from the studio to a nearby café. By the time we were seated, she was practically offering me a job. It looked like lunch was a good idea, and I had a feeling it was going to get even better. Hopefully she had the information I wanted.

We both ordered salads before we got down to the reason I was there.

"So, you gave me some names to check and see if they auditioned for us," Tilda said, taking notepaper from her purse. "We had a Mason Stone audition a couple of months ago."

"Why didn't he get it?" I asked.

"Well, that's just it," she said. "He did get the part."

"What?"

"Yeah," she said. "There were about a dozen men who came in for the part, and Mason Stone was our pick."

"So what happened?"

"All we know is we got word that he was dead," she said. "Somebody killed him."

"Then what happened?"

"We went with our second choice," she said, looking at her notes again. "Matt Lewis."

"Can I borrow some of that paper?" I asked.

"Sure."

She tore a piece in half and handed it to me. I wrote down Matt's name.

"Anything else you can tell me?" I asked.

"Well . . . there was something odd. I sat in for the actors' readings."

"And?"

"Well, another guy came to audition, and he brought his mother with him."

Just then the waitress walked up with our salads and iced teas. I took a sip of my drink before I said, "That's not that weird. I mean, sometimes you bring a relative or a friend to an audition. Maybe she was visiting?" I asked.

"No, this was weird: she was all over him, smoothing down his hair, pinching his cheeks, fixing his collar."

"So, a stage mom." I'd seen it before. This actor seemed a little older than most kids who have them, but I guess it happens.

"She gave new meaning to the phrase. We've all seen stage mothers and fathers. This was different. She was trying to ingratiate herself to the office staff, making sure we had his resume and head shot. She even pulled out some freshly baked cookies for the office staff! And the guy, I mean he's at least twenty-five years old and he's just letting her do this. His face was a blank. It was so . . . inappropriate. And she seemed desperate."

"Huh! That does sound weird. Poor guy." I looked at my watch. "By the way, I was hoping to stop over at *The Depths of the Sea* and talk to them about—"

Before I could finish, Tilda said, "They're dark today. They're taking some days off for summer vacation. Can you believe it? Some shows get all the breaks. Not us. We've been working on Saturdays lately. And eighteen-hour days." Well, that put a damper on any future employment possibilities. Yuck!

The waitress took our plates, adding, "Any dessert, ladies?"

"They have a really great cheesecake here," Tilda said conspiratorially.

"I'm sorry," I said to both of them, "but I have another appointment. I really don't have time. You go ahead."

"I think I will! I still have a little time left," Tilda said.

I thanked her and paid the check. As I was walking back to the studio to get my car, I pulled out my cell and called Jakes.

"Alex, how are you?"

I was happy to hear his voice. "I'm okay," I said, "thanks to you. You're my hero, you know."

He was quiet. I think I could hear him blushing.

"I like being your hero," he finally said. "When can I see you?"

"Actually, I have some answers for you and maybe a few questions," I said. "Where can we meet?"

"Have you had lunch?"

"Just."

"Coffee, then. Meet me at the same place we went last time, with Davis." He'd be able to walk there from Parker Center.

"Okay," I agreed. "Fifteen minutes?"

"Make it twenty."

"I'll be there," I said, and snapped the cell phone closed.

I got the Porsche started and headed for my meeting with Jakes.

Chapter 41

Jakes was sitting at a table with a glass of something in front of him. When he saw me he immediately got up. My heart was thumping out of my chest as he held my face in his hands and gently kissed me.

We sat down. I pulled my chair close to his.

"I've missed you," he whispered.

"I've missed you, too." We kissed a little more.

"Want some coffee?" He kissed my neck.

"What have you got?" I kissed his ear.

"Just a Coke." One more kiss.

"I'll have the same."

He waved a waitress over and ordered me a Coke while I sat and stared at him. She brought me my drink and then faded away.

"The eye doesn't look too bad," he said.

"I got a little haircut. It did the trick."

"I like it. It's sexy."

This whole thing was sexy. I shook it off. This was a public place after all.

"What about my car?" I asked. "When can I get it back?"

"Anytime," he said. "You'll need somebody to tow it, though."

"I'll have my garage guy get it."

"You have a regular guy to look after . . . that car?" he asked.

"No," I said, "my other car, but he'll come and get this one for me."

My mechanic's wife was a longtime soap fan. She would have made him come out in the middle of the night to get the car if I'd called.

"Okay," he said. "Just have him come to my office and I'll make sure he gets the keys. Now, do you have any other info for me?"

I took out the notepaper I'd written on and gave it to him. "Mason Stone got the job over at *The Best Days Are Ahead*, but he died before he could do even one episode."

"And who benefited from that?" he asked.

"That other name I wrote there, Matt Lewis."

Jakes frowned at the paper. "I guess I should look into Mr. Lewis, then. Thanks. What about the other show?"

"I've got a call in," I said, "and I'm still waiting to hear."

"Good," he said. "And what's this name? Eisenstein?"

"Oh," I said, "I remembered that this morning. He's the replacement on my show for Jackson Masters."

"Thank you, Alex," he said, giving me an appreciative look. He folded the note and put it in his pocket. "That's very helpful. Now, what about the other thing?"

"What other thing?"

"What we talked about," he said. "You know, about you backing off."

I hesitated.

"I knew it," he said. "You're too pissed to walk away, aren't you?"

"Wouldn't you be?"

"Yeah, but with me, having somebody try to kill me is an occupational hazard. If it bothered me enough, I'd stop being a cop."

"So, what would you do if you stopped being a cop, Jakes?"

"I'd probably die," he said.

I could tell he meant it. The job was everything to him. I didn't know what it would be like to have a man like that in my life. On a permanent basis, I mean.

"So you're not going to back off?" he said.

"No. At least, not until we find who killed Jackson and the others."

"And who tried to kill you."

"I think it'll come down to the same person, don't you?"

"Yes," he said, "I do."

"But why?" I asked. "And how come they didn't try to kill me the way they killed all the others? Strangling me somehow."

"I guess that's not part of the plan," Jakes said. "They want you out of the way not as part of the pattern, but because they think you know something. Do you?"

"Just what I've told you," I explained. "And certainly nothing that's worth killing me over."

"Maybe if you gave it some thought—"

"I have," I said. "I've been wracking my brain and

I can't figure it out. Why don't they try to kill you? Aren't you more of a danger than I am?"

"Apparently not," he said. "But there's also the fact that killing a cop is a bad idea. We hunt down cop killers forever."

"Yes, that would be a bad idea," I said, "but you don't mind if I worry about myself, just a little?"

"I want you to worry, Alex," he said. "I wish you would worry a hell of a lot!"

"Well," I promised him, "you're going to get what every man wants."

"What's that?"

"You're going to get your wish."

Chapter 42

As I got into my car, my cell phone sang out "Let's Talk About Sex," and I pushed the phone icon.

"Alex Peterson?" a man's voice asked.

"Speaking."

"Hey, Alex, this is Ross over at *The Depths of the Sea*."

"Ross, thanks for calling me back. How was your vacation?"

"Never long enough. I guess I should just be thankful we got a few days, right? The other shows—like yours—are working all year," he said. "I saw you at the Emmys. You looked awesome. Too awful about what happened."

"Yes, well, that's kind of why I called you, Ross," I said.

I explained to him that I was "assisting" the police in their investigation by gathering information about the parts the dead men had auditioned for.

"What? You mean, more were killed? Not just Jackson Masters?"

"That's not for public consumption, Ross," I said.

"If it gets out, you and I could both be in a lot of trouble with the cops."

"Oh, no, don't worry," Ross said, "I won't tell a soul."

"I'm looking for some information on an actor named Tom Nolan," I said. "I understand he auditioned for your show some time ago."

"That's what you said in your message, so I looked it up and you're right. He auditioned but wasn't what we were looking for."

"Who got it?"

"Michael Baze."

"He's cute," I said.

"That's one word for it!"

There was a billboard on Sunset Boulevard with Michael's substantial assets blown up for all the world to appreciate. He was an underwear model for a major designer.

"How did Tom Nolan react to not getting the part?" I asked.

"I don't know for sure. Disappointed, I guess." Then his tone changed. "But you'll find this funny. This other man who also auditioned? I couldn't believe this one."

"What do you mean?" I asked.

"I've seen a lot of nuts at readings, let me tell you. This one takes the cake," Ross said.

"Why?"

"He brought his crazy mother with him."

Chapter 43

I called my contacts at the other shows and then the associate producer at *The Yearning Tide*, deciding not to go through Andy again. I asked them all the same question and got the same answer.

I went home excited and found my kid car parked in front of the house, looking battered and bruised.

When I got inside I discovered that Jakes himself had accompanied it and stayed a while.

"Your mother was nice enough to offer me coffee," he said as I entered the kitchen.

"My mother has always been a very good hostess."

I smiled at Mom, and she smiled back.

"I have also always known when to get lost," she said. And discreetly left the room.

"Mom, you don't have to—" I started, but she was already gone.

"I hope she didn't leave because of me," Jakes said.

Was he kidding? I just looked at him and shook my head. Men can be so dense. "I have some news for you," I said. "Let me get myself a cup."

"You look like you're busting to tell me."

"I am."

I carried my coffee cup to the table and sat opposite him. I told him about my day, and the things I'd discovered, ending with the twenty-five-year-old actor who still had a pushy and crazy stage mother.

"So?"

"I heard the same thing from two people today," I said, "so I called the other two shows. And guess what?"

"What?"

"The same actor had auditioned for them, too . . . and his mother was with him."

"And?"

"What do you mean, 'and'?"

"Are you trying to say that this über–stage mother killed all four actors because her son didn't get a part he went out for?"

"It's too much of a coincidence, isn't it?"

"But, Alex, wouldn't she kill the actors who got hired ahead of her son? What's the point of targeting the men who have been killed? None of them were even working on a soap."

"Except Jackson."

"Right, except Jackson, but my point still stands. It was good thinking, Alex," he said, "but you know more about this stuff than I do. Wouldn't a pushy stage mother always be there?"

"For a child, yes," I said, "but this guy was twenty-five years old."

"And still attached to Momma's apron strings."

I sat back in my chair, feeling defeated.

"Don't feel bad, Alex," Jakes said. "I've had a million theories slapped down over the years."

He took a business card from his pocket and put it down on the table between us. "I know you have a mechanic, but he probably specializes in sports cars. This guy restores wrecks. Tell him I sent you."

"I will. Thanks."

He looked at his watch. "I've got to get going," he said, standing up. "Tell your mother thanks for the coffee."

"I will."

He grabbed my shoulders as he passed and pulled me to him, kissing me hard. I pulled away, looking around the room.

"Um, my mom . . ."

"Oh, yeah. Sorry." He kissed me again anyway before heading for the door. "Just out of curiosity, what's that actor's name? The one with the pushy mother?"

"His name's Nathan Russell."

"Russell," he said. "Thanks."

I sat where I was until the front door closed. I sipped my coffee and then jumped out of my seat and ran. I reached his car just as he was about to pull away and yanked open the passenger door.

"Alex, wha—"

"You almost got me, you faker," I said. "You like my theory. That's why you asked for the actor's name."

"Alex—"

"You're going to go and see this guy and his mother, aren't you?"

He hesitated and then said, "Just to ask a few questions, that's all."

"Well, you're not leaving me behind."

I got into the passenger seat and slammed the door behind me.

"I'm not going right now, Alex," he said. "Besides,

you can't just leave without telling your mom to pick Sarah up at camp."

"Damn," I said. He was right.

"Look," he said, "are you working tomorrow?"

"No," I said, giving him my most dejected look.

"I'll pick you up in the morning, and we'll go and talk to Nate and his mother."

"You're a shit, you know?" I said. "You were really going to do that without me? When I'm the one who found the lead?"

"The lead?" he said, smiling. "Yeah, you're right. It was your lead."

"Okay." I opened the door and put one foot out.

"But use some of that makeup you've got, change your face a little."

"Right."

"Maybe you could try disguising yourself as a stripper this time? Huh? Fishnets, patent leather boots?"

"Very funny!" I punched him on the shoulder and slammed his door. He was laughing as he drove off.

Chapter 44

Jakes picked me up nice and early and handed me a container of coffee as I got in the car.

"There ya go, partner," he said.

I opened the lid, took a look, closed it and sipped it.

"Just the way I like it."

We put our coffee in the holders between us. Our hands brushed only slightly but it was enough. We grabbed each other and went into a kiss. Breathless, I pulled away.

"Damn! We've got to control ourselves or we'll get nothing done!" I shook my head, trying to reach some degree of composure. "Where are we going?"

"Calabasas."

"Oh, the family must have money. Calabasas is nice."

"Not the nice Calabasas. The old Calabasas. Before all the developers took over. And the Kardashian girls."

"Did you call ahead?" I asked.

"No," he said, pulling away from the curb, "I didn't want to warn them."

"So what do we do if they're not home?"

"That's easy," he said. "We hear a noise inside, making it necessary for us to investigate."

"Break in?"

He grinned and said, "Only as a last resort."

We pulled up in front of an old ranch style house from the sixties. The "lawn" was a tired brown in dire need of watering. Or better yet, plowing. The sun was beating down on the concrete driveway, creating a glare that was blinding. Squinting, I managed to see a gray-haired, portly man about to get into a car. It was a Beamer, quite a few years old.

Jakes quickly got out of the car and I followed, first using the visor mirror to check that my wire-framed glasses, phony nose and front teeth were in place.

The man saw us coming and stopped at the car with his hand on the door.

"Can I help you?" he asked.

Jakes showed his ID. "Detective Jakes," he said. "This is my associate, Ms. Morgan. What's your name, sir?"

"Russell, Tim Russell. What's this about, Detective?"

"Actually," Jakes said, "I was looking for your wife, Adrienne."

"What did that crazy bitch do now?" the man demanded.

Jakes and I exchanged a glance.

"Look, we're divorced, have been for years," Russell said.

"What about Nate?" Jakes asked. "Is he around?"

"He doesn't live here, either," Russell said. "He moved out when she did."

"She got custody?"

"What custody?" the man asked. "He was twenty at the time."

"I don't understand."

"I never did, either," Russell said. "Those two were always close, you know? It was like they had a private club that I wasn't allowed to join."

A question sprang to mind, but I didn't ask it. I was supposed to let Jakes do the talking.

"Did she leave?" Jakes asked. "Or did you kick her out?"

"A little bit of both."

"And did you kick him out, too?"

"I told you," he said, "Nate was her little angel. He went where she went. As far as he's concerned she's a world-class stage mom."

"Mr. Russell, I'm going to ask you a question, and I don't want you to take a swing at me," Jakes said. "If you do I'll have to arrest you."

"Were they having sex?" Russell said. "Detective, I think they did everything together—but not that."

"How can you be so sure?"

"When you see my wife, you'll understand," he said. "She never was a very sexual person. And as for Nate—well, he's gay."

Russell was helpful after that. He gave us Adrienne Russell's home address and told us where Nate worked. He said if his wife got a job after she moved out, he didn't know about it.

We got in our car and moved on.

"I thought about the incest question," I said as Jakes drove, "and then you asked it."

"Great minds . . . ," Jakes said.

"Did you believe everything he said?" I asked.

"Yeah. Did you?"

"Yes, I did," I said. "I also admired his restraint."

"Meaning?"

"Most men would have bad-mouthed the wife a lit-tle more," I said. "Maybe even the kid. He seems . . . re-signed to it."

"He's moved on," Jakes said. "We better do the same."

Jakes wanted to talk to the kid first and then the mother. We drove to where he worked. The Cave was a sleazy dive where Nate tended bar. And they weren't kidding about the name. It was so dark I bumped into a barstool soon after walking in. When my eyes ad-justed to the "light," I saw it was the kind of place that makes you want to wash your hands as soon as you enter, and every other minute thereafter.

"Yeah, the kid works here, but he ain't been around for a few days."

"Did he have those days off?"

Nate Russell's boss mopped his bald head with a rag he pulled from his back pocket. I had a sick and disgusting feeling he used that same rag to dry his bar glasses.

"Naw, no days off," he said. "He was supposed to be workin', but guess what?"

"What?" Jakes asked.

"He can have all the days off he wants from now on," the man said. "He's freakin' history. And good riddance! Like I need a mama's boy pouring beers and shots."

"What do you mean, mama's boy?"

"His loony mother. Coming in here on his late nights yelling at me that her boy needed his sleep cuz he had to 'audition' in the morning. Pansy-ass kid. Good riddance!"

Jakes and I looked at each other.

"You got an address for him?" Jakes asked.

"Sure, hold on."

As the man went off to get the address, I said, "I thought he lived with his mother?"

"This way," Jakes said, "we double-check."

Chapter 45

We headed for Adrienne Russell's home, hoping we'd find her son, Nate, there, too.

"If he's not home and not at work, will that make him a suspect?" I asked.

"He's a suspect already, in my book," Jakes said.

"And the mother?"

"I've seen some weird relationships in my time," he said. "Women who have maintained control over their children no matter what age they are. And boys, in particular."

At that moment I was very glad I was the mother of a girl.

"So you think she's been directing him to murder these young men?" I asked.

"No, I don't believe it," he said. "But it's a theory."

"That's a horrible thought," I said. "I mean, they'd both have to be so . . . amoral."

"Believe me, it's very possible."

"So that would make it Nate who tried to force me off the road?"

He risked a quick look at me and then turned back

to the traffic he was negotiating us through. "Would you rather it be him and not Randy?" he asked.

"Well, of course," I said. "For my daughter's sake I hope her father didn't try to kill me. Have you located him yet?"

"He's in the country," he said, "but I don't know yet if he's actually in LA."

"If he is, can you arrest him?"

"For forcing you off the road? Not unless we can prove it."

"What about for stealing my money? I mean, he cleaned me out, Jakes."

He thought a moment and then asked, "Was it a joint bank account?"

"Well, yeah. I mean, we were married—"

"So either one of you could write checks, make deposits, make withdrawals?"

I felt my shoulders slump. This was the same song and dance I'd gone through with the police when it happened.

"I know, I know," I said. "It was his money as much as mine."

"You should've kept your own account, Alex—"

"I know!" I snapped. "Like he did, the bastard."

"He had his own bank account?"

"He sure did. He was squirreling money away every week and I knew nothing about it."

"What did he do for a living?"

"He was an investment banker."

"Successful?"

"Not as much as he would have liked. He had a few big clients, and he cleaned them all out, too, when he disappeared."

"And he still stole from you?" He shook his head. "What a piece of work."

"Yep, that's Randy," I said. "A piece of work."

"Unfortunately," Jakes said, "embezzling from his wife is not something we can arrest him for."

I felt the old anger coming back. When Randy had left three years ago, I could've killed him when I realized what he had done not only to me, but to his daughter. Of course, I realized I couldn't hurt my daughter's father. I knew I'd have to turn that anger into something positive, so I chose to concentrate on both my work and my daughter.

"I hope the driver wasn't Randy," I said, "but I also hope Randy gets what's coming to him."

There are houses in North Hollywood that have been around since the early twentieth century. Back then there was a housing boom to accommodate all the craftsmen and -women who were hired to work on the movies as set builders, crew members, hair and makeup people, set designers, et cetera, once the movie business got rolling in the twenties. Adrienne Russell lived in one of those old Spanish houses, the arched doorway covered with bright red bougainvillea and a neat brick walkway leading up to the front porch.

Jakes pulled up and cut the engine. "Same deal," he said. "I do the talking."

"I remember."

We got out and walked to the front door. Jakes rang the bell and we waited for someone to answer. I was wearing glasses and a little cotton in my nose to broaden it. The cotton would also serve to make my voice sound nasal. I didn't wear the phony teeth this time, in case somebody offered us cake. I also had a dark wig.

"How much of your life has been spent doing this?" I asked.

"Standing on someone's porch, waiting for them to answer the door? A lot. And then we never know what's going to be on the other side. Lots of times someone opens the door, takes one look at our faces or our IDs and starts running. And most of the time, they haven't even done anything."

"Then why do they run?"

"Because everybody feels guilty about something."

We heard the lock in the door turn and it started to open. I thought I was prepared for anything, but I wasn't quite prepared for Adrienne Russell.

Chapter 46

Adrienne Russell looked just like Mrs. Butterworth, from the syrup bottle. She had gray hair neatly wrapped up on top of her head in a bun, a pudgy face punctuated with soft, rosy cheeks and a plump body that was even sporting a floral apron! People had said she was crazy. But to me she looked anything but. I could see, however, why her ex-husband said she was not very sexual.

"Yes, may I help you?" she asked sweetly.

"Adrienne Russell?" Jakes asked.

"Yes? Most folks call me Addie, but, yes, I'm Adrienne," she replied.

He took out his ID. "Detective Jakes, LAPD. This is my associate, Ms. Peters." He held the *s* long enough for me to realize he'd almost said my real name.

She blinked a few times behind her bifocals, I guess appraising me for a moment. She finally decided not to ask for my ID.

"May we come in?" Jakes asked.

"Yes, yes, of course." She opened the screen door and stepped aside for us to walk in. "May I ask what this is about?"

"We'd like to ask you some questions about your son."

"Nate?"

I always wondered why people do that. If someone asks me how my daughter is, I don't say, "Sarah?" It's as if people have to prove they know their child's name before they answer the question.

"What about my dear sweet boy? He hasn't been in a car accident, has he? Kids drive so fast these days!" She had her hand over her heart.

"No, no, nothing like that."

"Oh, thank heavens! I almost fainted! Come into the dining room," she said. "You'll have to excuse me; I'm a little busy."

"We appreciate your time," he said.

We followed her down the hallway past various end tables graced with lace doilies and vases filled with plastic flowers. Knickknacks adorned the shelves that lined the walls and every other available space. The farther we walked, the richer grew the smell of pot roast. When we got to the dining room, we saw what she had been busy with. The antique dark wood table was covered with a large lace table cloth. On top of that rested a mountain of resumes and photos of her son, Nate.

"Excuse the mess," she said. "We just got Nate new head shots."

"Head shots?" Jakes asked.

"My son, Nate, is an actor," she said proudly. "He's going to be a star."

I walked to the table and picked up a resume. It gave Nate Russell's birth year as 1983. If he was twenty-five, then he was definitely a "late in life" baby. Addie had to be sixty-five at least, if she was a day.

"Would you like a photo?" she asked me, holding one out proudly. "Isn't he just such a beautiful boy? He reminds me of a young Tyrone Power. Oh! He was the most adorable baby. And sweet! What a disposition. He never cried, never got fussy."

"Yes, he's handsome," I said, accepting the picture. "You must be very proud."

"Oh, I am," she said. "That's why I work so hard for him. My husband never understood that." She busied herself with stacking the manila envelopes. "Did he send you here?"

"Why would you ask that?" Jakes asked.

"Well, somebody gave you my address," she said with a shrug. "It was him, right? My biggest regret in life. That man! If only we could have stayed married. At least for Nate's sake! Lord knows, I tried." She looked at me and I swear she had a tear in her eye. "Sorry!" She reached for a tissue in a doily covered tissue box. "Some things are still so fresh, you know. I just never saw myself being a divorcée!"

"Was this a recent divorce?" I had to ask, given her response.

"Oh, heavens! No! It's been five years this Christmas! Ahhh!" She sighed, "I can only imagine what he must have told you about me and Nate."

When Jakes didn't offer anything, she continued looking at me. I didn't want to risk his wrath, so I said nothing. I'd probably already said too much.

"Has he had any success as an actor?" Jakes asked. "Nate, I mean."

"Some," she said. "He's auditioned for most of the daytime dramas, but . . ."

"But what?" he asked.

"They didn't seem to appreciate what he has to

offer," she said. "That's why I'm continuing to send out his resume and photo. Somebody will see it, I'm sure. I know, I know, all mothers think their children are special, but Nate truly is. Did you know he can sing? And dance! He even does accents!"

She seemed beyond determined to me but not at all bitter about all the rejection Nate had suffered.

"Well, if Natey isn't hurt," she said, "what can I do for you, Detective?"

"Do you know where Nate is?"

"At work, I assume."

"We went to his job. He wasn't there."

"Oh, that," she said, waving it off. "It's just temporary. Did you talk to that Neanderthal boss he works for?"

"Yes, we did."

"He's a horrible man." She sat down at the table and started stuffing resumes and pictures into the manila envelopes. "Why do you want to see Nate?"

"We're investigating some murders," Jakes said. "All the victims are young actors who resemble Nate."

She stopped what she was going. "Are you telling me Nate is in danger?"

"Could be." Jakes jumped on that right away. If she thought we were thinking of Nate in terms of being another victim, she might talk more openly.

"My God," she said. "Wait, was that one of the murders that happened on the Daytime Emmy Awards a few weeks ago?"

"Yes, it was."

"How many murders have there been?"

"Five, so far."

She sat back in her chair and let her hands fall into

her lap. Suddenly I wondered if she had ever done any acting herself. It was something to look into later.

One benefit of being in the business is you can almost always tell when somebody's acting—whether they're doing it badly or well. In Adrienne Russell's case, I had the feeling she was doing it very well.

"This is awful," she said. "Will I have to stop sending Nate out on auditions?"

"Well," Jakes said, "nobody's yet been killed while out on an audition."

"That's good news."

"Does Nate have an agent?" Jakes asked.

She smiled and said, "You're looking at her. I know I'm not exactly ICM or CAA, but nobody believes in him like I do.

"And if you're thinking of me as a stage mother, I'm here to tell you I'm much more than that."

That much was obvious.

"I've sacrificed a lot for Nate," she said. "But it will all come back to me in the end."

I wondered if it all came back to her, would she give any to Nate?

Chapter 47

"What kind of a hostess am I?" Adrienne asked. "Would you like some tea or coffee or a cold drink?"

"No, nothing, thanks," Jakes said.

I shook my head and caught her looking at me funny.

"Do I know you?" she asked. "I mean, have we met before?"

I fidgeted behind my disguise. "I don't believe so," I said.

"You look so familiar."

"Mrs. Russell—" Jakes said.

"Addie, please."

"Addie, do you know where Nate is right now?"

"Oh! Goodness! I forgot all about my pot roast!" And she shuffled into the kitchen. "I have gotten so forgetful! Sweet Jesus, Mary and Joseph!"

Jakes and I looked at each other. I was about to mouth, "Do you think she's for real?" when Addie popped her head around the dining room door.

"You know, normally I know where he is every minute of the day."

"But not now?" Jakes asked.

"Right at this minute? No."

"Doesn't that worry you?"

"Well, it wouldn't have, normally, but now that you've told me he may be in danger, I am worried, yes."

"Here's my card," Jakes said, handing her one. "If you happen to locate him, would you let me know?"

"Of course, Detective," she said. "And I imagine you're going out to look for him now?"

"If we can."

"Please let me know if you find him before I do."

"Of course."

"I'll start making calls right away," she said with a smile. "You know, to Nate's girlfriends. He has so many."

Either she was in denial about Nate being gay, or she was lying . . . or Mr. Russell had lied. I wondered how Jakes could live his life like this, day in, day out, trying to figure out who was lying and who was telling him the truth.

"You might as well call his boyfriends, too," Jakes said. "I mean, his buddies."

"I'll do that," she said. "I'll call . . . everyone. Shall I see you out?" For an ever so brief moment I thought I detected a darkness wash over her face. Overactive imagination? I wasn't sure.

She walked us to the door and stood pulling at her apron strings. Her nerves were starting to show.

"Thank you for your time, Addie," Jakes said.

"Not at all, Detective," she said. "Thank you for the warning."

She looked at me. "I still can't help feeling we know each other."

I just nodded. I didn't want to risk my voice giving me away.

Jakes took my arm and guided me outside. By the time we reached the car, Adrienne Russell had closed her front door.

"She almost made you," he said after we got into the car.

"I was telling the truth," I said. "We haven't met. She probably thinks she knows me because she's seen me on television. So, what did you think of her?" I asked.

"Well, on the surface she's a sweet, older woman intent on making her son a star. Still a stage mom, in my book, as much as she'd like to call herself an agent. What did you think?"

"She was acting."

"Which part?"

"All of it, I think," I said, "She's very good at innocent little old lady, but it just didn't ring true. Especially her concern about Nate being in danger."

"He can't be in danger of being killed if she's his accomplice to murder."

"Tell me," I said, "what chance do we have of finding Nate before she does when we have no idea where to look?"

"But I do have an idea," he said.

"Where?"

"Here."

"You're going on a stakeout?"

"Care to join me? They're boring as hell, but maybe we could find a way to pass the time."

I knew exactly what he meant, and Lord knows, I was tempted. "I can't. I'd love to but I want to spend some serious time with Sarah."

"Gotcha. Um, I should stay here, so how do we get you home?"

"George lives ten minutes away. Could you drop me off there? I'm sure he or Wayne could take me home."

"Let's go!" He pulled out onto the freeway, heading toward Silver Lake. "But I still want to kill some time with you. Not necessarily on a stakeout."

Chapter 48

When I got home, I could smell dinner cooking. Again I felt guilty that my mother had been doing all the housework since she got back home. Even though I had to work on my show, I tried to do as much at home as I could. Except, of course, when I was trying to find a killer.

"Hi, Mom," I said, entering the kitchen and kissing her. "I'm sorry you have to make dinner again."

"I don't mind pitching in, Alex," she said, "until things get back to normal. Any idea when that would be?"

"Soon, Mom. Very soon."

"Well, Sarah's in her room."

"All right."

I had to go and say hi to my baby girl, stopping first in the bathroom to remove my makeup. I heard every word she said as she told me about her day.

"Here, dear," my mother said, handing me a glass of white wine as I reentered the kitchen.

"Mom, would you kill someone for me?" I asked.

"Why, who do you want me to kill?"

"I'm serious, Mom."

She turned away from the stove and looked at me. "I can see you are. Well, Alex, a mother's love is very strong. You know that. I would kill to protect you, just as you would to protect Sarah."

"Yes," I said, "to save her, I would. But . . ."

"But what?"

"We found out that the same actor has auditioned for the parts some of the dead men got. Not all, but some. And he always had his mother with him."

"Are you wondering if she killed all those men to get her son a part in a TV show?"

"It's possible, Mom, except for one thing."

"What's that?"

"He didn't get the parts," I said. "Why would she kill them if he didn't get the parts anyway?"

"I think you need to go over these things with your friend the detective," she said.

"I think you're right."

The doorbell rang at that moment.

My mom winced. "Oh, dear. I forgot to tell you. Paul called and said he'd be dropping by this evening."

"Mother!"

"I'm sorry," she said.

Maybe it wasn't Paul, I thought on my way to the door. Maybe it was Jakes. Please . . . make it be Jakes.

When I opened the door, Paul Silas was standing there. We hadn't spoken since I had told him not to come home after the Emmys.

"Paul."

"Hello, Alex. Could you step out here, please?"

The fact that he wanted to talk outside, and didn't try to kiss me hello, spoke volumes.

I walked outside, closed the door and turned to face him. "When did you get back?" I asked.

"Yesterday."

"Paul—"

"Let me say something first."

"Okay. Uh . . . do you want to go somewhere?"

"No, actually I don't. I just didn't want to see Sarah." It looked like he was tearing up a little. He turned away from me for a second before he sighed and said, "Let's just keep this simple and to the point. You're involved in solving a murder again," he said, "like last year, right?"

"Well . . . I did have Jackson's body almost fall on me. . . ."

"And that means you're probably seeing Detective Jakes again."

I wasn't going to disrespect what I had had with Jakes by denying it. "Paul . . . I'm sorry. I don't know what to say. It's not you, it's m—"

"Whatever you say, please don't give me that old line! Look, I need more from a woman and a relationship. The trouble is I love you, Alex. I've told you that many times. I don't think you've said it to me more than twice and probably because you felt you had to."

"I do care about you, Paul. You're an amazing man." I meant it, too. I was at a loss. I wanted to say something profound, but I felt paralyzed. I opened my mouth but nothing came out.

"I get it," he said. "And you know what? It's okay. We met shortly after your marriage ended. I guess I was rebound man." He looked me square in the eyes and said, "I'm going to miss you, and almost worse than anything, I'm going to miss Sarah." He stifled a sob and I felt myself welling up.

"I am so sorry, Paul. I don't know why I couldn't make it work for me with you." I was tempted to reach out to him but thought that would be too much. "You're probably right. If it's not going to work for us, it's better to end it now before Sarah gets too attached to you."

"Yeah." He looked down and composed himself before saying, "Look, just cuz we didn't work out that way doesn't mean, you know . . . I guess what I'm trying to say is if you need anything, call me. I know you too well. Please don't do anything stupid, Alex, with this whole murder investigation business."

"I'd say I won't, but I don't want to be a liar!" I was trying for a little levity. "Maybe, um, after some time has gone by, maybe you could come by and see Sarah? She loves you. I know it would mean a lot to her."

I guess that was too much to hear because he just nodded his head and started down the walk. "You take care, Alex. I'll call you." He turned away and walked out of my life. I couldn't help but be sad. Another one bites the dust. I stood there, stunned at how easy it had seemed but at the same time filled with remorse because I hadn't had the courage to end it myself in a better way. To admit what was obvious from the first time I'd met Frank Jakes—that I was never in love with Paul, and that I was attracted to Jakes right from the beginning.

"Was that Paul?" my mother asked as I walked into the kitchen.

"Yes, it was."

"He's not staying for dinner?" She looked at me closely.

"No, Mom, he's not," I said.

"Are you okay?"

"Not entirely. But I will be."

She put her spoon down, came over and wrapped her arms around me. Even though I hadn't been in love with Paul, it still felt like a loss. And I cried.

"It's okay, sweetheart. After all, love isn't for wimps."

I laughed out loud and, wiping my eyes, said, "It sure as hell isn't!"

Chapter 49

The next morning Jakes called as I was making breakfast for all of us.

"Can I come and pick you up?" he asked. "We got another one."

I went cold. "Another what?"

"Body."

"Oh, God."

"The victim fits the description of the others," he said. "No ID on him, though. I'd like to see if you know him from your soaps."

I looked at my mother, who waved at me to go. Mother-daughter ESP at work.

"All right," I said. "Pick me up."

"Okay."

"Wait! Did you get to talk to Nate last night?"

"I'll tell you about that when I pick you up."

I hung up.

"Go get dressed," Mom said. "I'll fix Sarah some breakfast, and she can stay home from surf camp today."

"Thank you, Mom."

* * *

I was waiting out front when Jakes pulled up. I had called into work to tell them I'd be unavoidably late. They would tape around me as much as they could. I hopped into the passenger seat and we were off.

He told me what happened while he was on stakeout the day before:

It was just after dark when a car pulled into the driveway and a young man got out and started for the front door. Jakes got out of his car and ran up behind him.

"Excuse me," Jakes said, holding out his ID.

The younger man turned around and looked startled when he saw Jakes. "Who are you? Whaddya want?"

"Take it easy. My name's Detective Jakes. I just want to talk to you. That is, if you're Nate Russell?"

"I am," he said. He looked behind him at the house, maybe checking to see if anyone was coming out. "Can we talk out here? I don't want to worry my mom. She gets kind of jumpy."

Jakes didn't think he'd ever met a less jumpy woman than Adrienne Russell, but he kept it to himself.

Jakes knew he couldn't ask Nate Russell to account for his whereabouts on the five dates that the men had been killed. Civilians didn't normally keep track of their comings and goings that closely. But he could ask him where he was when Jackson was killed, and then again when Henri Marceau was killed.

"And what were those days?" Nate asked.

Jakes repeated them. "Come on, Nate," he added. "It wasn't that long ago."

"Well, I'd say I was either at an audition or at work."

"Gotta be more specific than that, Nate."

"I can't—"

"Maybe if we go downtown you'll be able to remember more," Jakes said, grabbing his arm.

"No!" he shouted, just as the light went on next to the front door and Adrienne Russell appeared.

"What's going on?" she demanded.

"Nothing," Jakes said. "I was just asking your son some questions he can't seem to answer."

"He's arresting me, Ma!"

"I'm not arresting him," Jakes said. "I'm taking him in for questioning."

"What questions are you asking him?" she demanded. "I'm sure I can help."

"I doubt it, ma'am," Jakes said. "You couldn't tell me where he was today. How are you going to tell me where he was on the days of the murders?"

"I told him, Ma, I was either at an audition or at work," Nate yelled, still trying to pull free from Jakes's hold.

"Let him go!" she said. "I can give you the answers."

"Can you?" Jakes reluctantly released Nate's arm.

"It's all in my book," she said. "Nate, go to my room and get my book off my dresser."

"Your book?"

"Yes," she said, "the appointment book I keep all your auditions in."

"Oh, that book."

Nate went into the house. . . .

"Oh, Jakes." I closed my eyes.

"I know," he said, keeping his eyes on the road. I

think he was ashamed to look at me. "I screwed up big-time."

"Did you look—"

"I looked for him," he said. "He obviously ducked out the back door."

"What about the mother?"

"She kept me busy out front. I guess I could've arrested her," he said.

"Then why didn't you?"

"I put a man on her," he said. "She's all Nate has. If he tries to contact her or if she tries to meet him, we'll know."

"And that book she was talking about?"

"There was no book."

"Wait," I said. "This murder we're going to now . . . how could she be involved if she's being watched?"

"She's either in the clear on this one," he said, "or she got it done before I put a tail on her. Which means she had to have had it planned a while to pull it off in that short a time."

"But that's only if this murder is the same as the others, right?"

"Right."

"Have you been there yet?"

"No," he said. "I got the call and immediately I called you."

"What about your partner?"

"He's going to meet me there."

"What if it's not connected?" I asked.

"I hope it is," he said. "It'll give us something fresh to work on."

"Wow, that's . . . terrible," I said, "but so . . . true."

Chapter 50

As we pulled up to the crime scene, I asked, "Was your man in front of my house last night?"

"Of course."

"Then you know I had a visitor last night."

"I heard," he said. "I assumed it was Paul."

"It was."

He put his hand over mine, a gesture that I found both touching and comforting.

"Was it hard for you?"

"Actually, no," I said. "I mean, I was expecting a soap opera–esque breakup, but he made it very easy— easier than I deserved."

"Don't think about it," he said. "It's over. Now we have to move on."

He looked past me out the window at the house that was surrounded by both cops and yellow crime scene tape.

"Let's go then," I said, unbuckling my seat belt.

I could tell by the look Detective Davis gave Jakes that he didn't approve of my presence.

"We got a young man named Ben Tillman," Davis said. "He was an actor."

"Is he the same type as the others?" Jakes asked.

"Yup." Finally Davis couldn't contain himself. "Why is she here?"

"If the deceased is connected to soap operas, Alex will know," Jakes told him.

Davis grudgingly looked at me. "Hello, Ms. Peterson."

"Detective."

"He's in here."

David led us into the house, into a high-ceilinged living room that had wooden beams. The young man was hanging by the neck from one of the beams.

"Can we cut him down?" a man from the crime lab asked.

"Give me a minute," Jakes said. "Alex? Why don't you wait outside?"

"I—I'm fine," I said. "You asked me to come." I didn't want him to think I was weak.

"Okay," he said.

He surveyed the room, taking it all in, and walked around a bit, hardly looking at the body. Me, I couldn't take my eyes off the poor man. His eyes were closed, his swollen tongue protruded from his mouth, but there was no blood.

Jakes now looked around, searching for something or someone in particular. "Doc?"

An older man wearing a white coat came forward. I guessed he was the medical examiner.

"What's wrong with this picture?" Jakes asked, looking up at the dead man.

"You mean the tongue?"

"Am I right that if he hanged himself, his neck

would have broken? There'd be no reason for the tongue to be out like that."

"You're right," the doctor said. "That's a high beam. If he'd done this himself, his neck would've broken. The tongue hanging out is an indication that he suffocated."

"If he hanged himself," I asked, "where's the chair or stool he would've had to stand on?"

"She's right," Jakes said. "Whatever he climbed on to get up there would still be around."

The floor beneath him was bare.

"Murder," Jakes said. "Nice call, Alex."

I felt queasy but proud.

"I'll know more after I cut him down," the ME said.

"What are you waiting for?" Jakes asked.

The ME turned to his men and said, "Cut him down!"

Jakes came over to me. "Do you know him?" he asked.

"It's hard to say with his tongue protruding like that," I said. "He certainly resembles Jackson and the others. What are the differences from the other cases?"

"If this is his home . . . ," he said, looking over at Davis, who nodded, "then he was killed where he lives. None of the others were."

He meant none of the other actors. Henri was killed at home.

"I see."

"Do you want to wait outside?"

"No," I said, "I'd like to get a closer look at him, and then I'll step outside."

"Okay."

I watched as it took three men to cut the young man down, but eventually they had him lying on the floor. I moved closer. His tongue was still disfiguring his face, making it hard to see what he truly looked like. I was about to bend over when a voice called out sharply, "What is she doing here?"

I turned my head and saw Jakes's boss standing in the doorway, looking furious.

"Captain Carpenter—" Jakes started.

"Officer," she snapped at a nearby uniformed cop, "please escort Ms. Peterson from the premises."

"Yes, Captain."

"And I mean behind the crime scene tape!"

"Yes, si—uh, Captain."

"Now wait a minute," Jakes said. "This is my crime scene—"

"That may be true, Detective," the captain said, "but I believe I still outrank you."

I was escorted away without her ever speaking directly to me and without my being able to say anything to Jakes.

Chapter 51

I wasn't sure where to go. Should I leave the scene completely? Or just stay away from the house? Should I go home? Go to work? How would I do either? Get a ride from someone? Take the bus?

I decided to wait for Jakes in the front seat of his car. It took hours. I didn't have his keys so I couldn't turn on the air-conditioning or crack the windows. I had to sit with the passenger door open so I wouldn't suffocate. With the door open, I could hear shouting from inside the house.

I watched the ME come out, watched his people load the body into a van and drive away.

Then uniformed cops came out. Some drove away in their marked cars; others started going door-to-door. Eventually Detective Davis also came out and started going door-to-door.

When Captain Carpenter finally came out, I pulled the door shut and ducked down so she wouldn't see me. I felt like a little kid, but I didn't know what else to do. This chick was mean. And clearly she didn't like me. When I heard a car drive away, I sneaked a peek. I saw that she was gone, so I opened the door again and sat with my feet out.

Just when I was thinking I could use a cup of coffee, Jakes came out. It was past noon. He looked disheveled, as if he'd been up all night. He hadn't looked that way when he picked me up.

He came over to the car and got in, showing no surprise that I was there.

"Should I take you home or to work?" he asked.

"Neither," I said. "Take me someplace for a late breakfast, so we can talk. I'm starving."

He looked at me, started to say something and then stopped. Finally he said, "Okay. Breakfast it is."

He pulled over at the first diner we came to. He ordered a stack of pancakes; I had eggs Benedict.

"His name is Ben Tillman. That name ring a bell?"

"No."

"We found stuff in the house that tells us he's an actor. He had a SAG card in his wallet and a drawer full of head shots. He had two DVDs of movies he's been in."

"How long ago?"

"Five, six years," Jakes said. "Coming of age stuff. Nothing since."

"How was he killed?"

"He was strangled first and then strung up."

"By somebody strong."

"Or more than one person."

"You think Adrienne or Nate went out last night and killed him after they talked with you?"

Jakes shook his head. "ME says he'd been dead at least thirty-six hours."

"So somebody killed him and strung him up the day before yesterday."

"Well before we talked to the Russells."

"Do you think that's why Nate ran?"

He shrugged.

"Are you going to bring his mother in?"

"I can't," he said. "The captain won't let me. Says we don't have any probable cause."

"She still doesn't believe that you have one killer for all these murders?"

"She says she needs more than my hunch."

"What about your partner?" I asked. "Doesn't he back you up?"

"No."

"But—"

"She also dressed me down in front of everyone for having you there."

"I figured that," I said. I reached out and touched his hand. "I don't want to do anything that will hurt you, Jakes."

"I know," he said.

"It seems to me you could avoid a lot of trouble with your boss if you just kept me out of things. I'm beginning to think you like . . . rubbing me in her face."

He turned his hand over, closed it around mine. "There was never anything between me and her, Alex," he said. "You have to believe that."

"Then why is she riding you? She looked at me like a jealous woman looks at a rival."

"She might be jealous—who knows?" he asked. He released my hand so we could both continue eating. "But I haven't given her any cause to be. Besides, this is old news for you and me. There's no reason to talk about her anymore."

I studied his face, searching for any insincerity. I didn't see any. He picked at his pancakes. "This is still my case, and now that there's been another murder, she can't pull me off."

"Why not?"

"There's just too much background for someone else to catch up on."

"What about Davis?"

"He's the only logical choice, but he wouldn't take my case," he told me.

"Why?"

"Because he's my partner."

Something was wrong. He wasn't meeting my eyes.

"And what about me?"

He looked at me this time. "She said she doesn't want to see you at any more crime scenes."

"That's all she said?"

He nodded.

"Well," I said, "we can do that."

He smiled. "Yeah," he said. "We can."

Chapter 52

As he drove me to the studio, I said, "I have a question."

"What?"

"Is there another son?"

"Sorry?"

"Adrienne Russell," I said. "Does she have another son? Does Nate have a brother?"

He hesitated a moment and then said, "You know, I never asked."

"If Adrienne Russell is behind these murders, she'd need help."

"And you don't think that would be Nate?"

"I don't know," I said. "I didn't talk to him. You did. Do you think he's a killer?"

His right hand closed into a fist, but I was glad he didn't use it. He just squeezed it hard. "I let him get away, so I didn't have a lot of time with him." He took a quick look at me. "I'll check and see if he has any other family."

"What about the husband?" I asked. "Do you think he might help her?"

"No," Jakes said. "Him I believed. He's too bitter to be helping her kill people."

"I'm going to check Adrienne out when I get to work," I said.

"How do you mean?"

"I mean, I want to check and see if she was ever an actress."

"You think she's trying to live through her son because she couldn't succeed?'

"Could be. Maybe she's so driven to make him a success because she never became one. It's that way with a lot of stage mothers."

"That sounds like a good idea," Jakes said. "Let me know what you find out."

When the guard saw me in the passenger seat, he waved Jakes on through. I had originally asked him to drive me home so I could get my car, but he said he'd pick me up when I finished with work. I was amazed at how comfortable I already felt with him—a level of comfort I had never been able to achieve with Paul.

It was even evident when he leaned over to kiss me good-bye.

"Have a good day at work," he said. "Call me when you're done and I'll pick you up."

"I will."

I got out and watched as he drove away, and then turned and went into the building.

The first person I ran into was the director, Richard Breck.

"Hey, Dick, I'm sorry—"

"Save it, Alex," he said, holding up a hand. "Sean wants to see you. Now."

That didn't sound good. "Do you know what it's about?"

"Hey, they don't confide in me," Dick said. "Just do me a huge favor and get on the set as soon as possible?"

"Okay, Dick. Thanks."

I wondered if I was in as much trouble with one of my bosses as Jakes was with his.

I made my way to Sean Peters's office. As I entered he was on the phone. He held up one finger to me, and I stood there and waited.

"Sorry about that," he said, hanging up several minutes later. "I had to finish that call."

"I understand. You wanted to see me?"

"I did," he said. "Alex, what's going on?"

"How do you mean?"

"You've been coming in late, calling in late, forcing us to tape around you . . . ever since that incident at the Emmys. Are you all right?"

"I'm fine, Sean."

He stood up, came around the desk, touched his hair and then put his arm around me. "Because if you need some time off, just tell me. We'll arrange it."

I could have felt touched at that moment, but I was suspicious. Here I thought he was going to call me on the carpet, and instead he was being incredibly sensitive. That wasn't like Sean Peters at all.

"I know what a shock you had—"

"That was two weeks ago, Sean," I said. "I'm fine, really."

"Really?"

"Yes."

He patted my shoulder and then removed his arm.

Suddenly, the look on his face changed. "Then what the hell is going on with you, Alex?" he demanded.

"I—Sorry?"

"You've been late, you're forcing us to tape around you. . . . Why?"

I felt like we were having the same conversation but with him in an entirely different mood.

"I mean, I know you're Alex Peterson—I get that," he said. "You're one of the queens of daytime. I get that, too. But I've never thought of you as a diva, Alex."

"Neither have I, Sean—"

"Then why are you acting like that?" he demanded. "I don't know how it was on *Yearning Tide*, Alex, but here on *B and B* everybody carries their weight."

I wanted to be indignant, I wanted to shout at him, but I couldn't because he was right. Not that I'd been acting like a diva, but in agreeing to help Jakes with his investigation—by *wanting* to be involved—I had been pushing my job to the back burner. That certainly wasn't fair to the rest of the cast or the crew.

"I understand, Sean," I said. "To tell you the truth, I've have been rather . . . shaky since Jackson almost fell on me, since I was covered with his blood . . ."

I felt bad. The look on Sean's face changed. Once again becoming solicitous, he put his arm around me.

"I knew it," he said. "I know you're a rock, Alex, but something . . . horrible like that . . . it has to have a lasting effect."

"I'm doing okay, really . . . most of the time. . . ."

"Do you want some time off?"

"No, no, Sean," I said, "I don't. I'll be all right, really. I'm here to work."

He patted my shoulder and said, "You're a trouper, Alex. But if you need some time off, please let me know . . . in advance, so I can schedule around you."

"I—I'll do my best, Sean."

"Good," he said. "Good. Now . . . get to work."

I left, knowing that I deserved a Daytime Emmy for my time in his office, and feeling both bad about it . . . and just a little satisfied. I was afraid he was going to make me choose between my job and the investigation. I would have had to pick my job, of course.

But as I made my way to my dressing room, I felt a kinship with Jakes. We were two mavericks, flying in the face of authority to solve these murders.

I'd never been a maverick before.

Chapter 53

I focused all my concentration on my scenes that day, but luckily I had only three, so that wasn't very hard to do. It was after my scenes were over that the day turned.

I entered my dressing room and saw an envelope with my name on it sitting on the dressing table. My heart almost stopped when I recognized the chicken scratch. Only one person I knew had that immature handwriting. I tore the envelope open and pulled out a note written in the same scribble:

> *Hey, Babe.*
> *Don't worry about Sarah. I'll pick her up today from camp, take her out for dinner, and then bring her home later. Can't wait to see you.*
> *Love,*
> *Randy*

I admit it. I panicked. I ran out of my dressing room and went looking for a crew member, a stage manager, someone. I needed to find out if anyone had seen who had left the note in my dressing room. If it was Randy himself, then he'd found some way past the guards and into the building without a pass—or he'd convinced someone to give him a pass.

I talked to several people, who either saw nothing or admitted nothing in the face of my obvious distress. I decided to take it to Sean Peters.

I found him in his office, sitting behind his desk and again on the phone. I could tell from his end of the conversation that he wasn't discussing business. I was too harried to wait for him to finish his personal call, so I slammed my hand down on the receiver, cutting the connection.

"Alex, what the—"

"Read this!" I thrust the note into his face.

He took it, read it quickly, and then looked at me. It took a moment for it to dawn on him.

"Wait," he said, "this is your ex—"

"Yes," I said, "the man who abandoned me and my daughter and stole all of my money. The man who's been missing for years. A man who has no right to be on these premises."

"Okay, Alex," he said, standing up. Despite the conversation, he remembered to touch his hair—and despite the conversation, I managed to notice. "Take it easy—"

"Take it easy?" I asked. "Sean, I want to know how this note got in my dressing room. I want to know how he got into the building, let alone on the lot. If you think I've been upset up to now, you ain't seen nothing yet." I grabbed the note back and crumpled it in my hand. "If I see Randy, I can't be responsible for what I'm gonna do to him. This man abandoned my little girl, and now he thinks he's going to come back into her life—and into *my* life? Goddamn it—"

"Alex, Alex!" he said.

I stopped abruptly, realizing I was a millimeter from being completely out of control.

"I'll look into it," he said. "I'll find out how the note got here. I swear. Leave it to me. Go take care of your daughter."

I took a deep breath. "Sean . . . I'm sorry I shouted at you."

"Not at all," he said. "You get yourself home and I'll look into this. When I find out who let him into the building, I'll have their job and their head."

"Thank you, Sean."

I left his office and walked back to my dressing room—even though I wanted to run. When I got there I called Jakes.

Jakes pulled up in front of the building and I ran to the car.

"Let me see the note," he said.

"Is your man still on Sarah?" I asked.

"Yes," he said. "I just spoke to him. He's with your mother and her."

"He didn't upset my mother, did he? Or Sarah?"

"No, Alex, everything's fine," he said. "Give it to me."

"What does it matter?" I asked, but I handed the note to him.

"You crumpled it?"

"I was . . . crazed!" I said.

"Okay, okay," he said. "It doesn't matter. You're sure this is Randy's handwriting?"

"It looks like a second grader wrote it, doesn't it? That's him."

"Alex, I'm sorry—"

"What are you sorry about?"

"I've been concentrating so hard on the murders . . . and on us. . . . I should have found him by now."

"Don't apologize to me, Jakes," I said. "So far you've saved my life once. You get a pass—"

"No," he said, "I don't want a pass. I'm going to find this bastard and make him pay for what he's done to you."

"I don't want you to shoot him," I said.

"I won't shoot him," he said, starting the car. "I'll lock his ass up."

"Good."

We had driven past the guardhouse and pulled out onto the street when I said, "I want to shoot him myself."

Chapter 54

When we got to my house, Jakes came inside with me after waving to his man across the street. Sarah and my mom were there. I gave my little girl a long hug, one she wiggled out of after a while.

"I have to go play in my room, Mommy," she said, and hustled away.

"Detective," my mom said. "Can I offer you something? Coffee? Something stronger?"

"Coffee would be nice, Mrs. Peterson."

Mom started for the kitchen and then stopped and turned back. "I'm making dinner," she said to Jakes. "Would you like to join us? There's plenty."

He looked at me, but I left it entirely up to him.

"Unless you have a previous engagement?" My mother raised her eyebrows. "Someone waiting for you at home?"

"No," he said, "nobody waiting for me. Dinner sounds great."

"Good."

While Mom went back into the kitchen, Jakes looked at me and said, "I'm going to go across the street and tell Kavanaugh to take a break."

"Okay. I'm going to take a shower and put something else on."

Dinner went off without a hitch. The conversation was lively, especially between Jakes and my mother. Everything was fine until Sarah made a perfectly innocent faux pas.

"Mommy, where's Paulie?" she asked.

All the adults at the table looked at one another, and then two of them looked at me. "This one's yours," their faces said.

"I'm not really sure, honey," I said, hedging.

She asked the next question the way most children do, without looking up at anyone in particular. Her eyes were intent on her French fries as she asked, "When is he coming back? I miss him."

I was tongue-tied. Thankfully Jakes stepped in just in time.

"I bet you do, Sarah. Your mom said he's a good friend of yours."

"Yeah, he's really nice. He reads to me a lot. He has lots of funny voices and stuff."

I couldn't help myself; I started to tear up.

"Well, I might not read quite as well as Paulie, but maybe sometime, I could try to read a book to you. You know, if you want." Jakes was speaking softly to her, looking her in the eyes.

"Yeah, that would be okay. Maybe even later, after dinner! I got a new book when I was at the r'union!"

Sure enough, after dinner Jakes read to Sarah, funny voices and all. He did remarkably well for someone who didn't have kids of his own.

"Time for bed," my mother said finally. "Say good night to Jakes, Sarah."

"Night, Jakes," Sarah said, waving.

"Good night, Sarah."

As she and my mom started from the living room, Sarah turned her head and said to me, "I like Jakes, Mommy, but he has a funny name."

Jakes just looked at me. "Yes, I do. Don't I, Sarah? Good night. it was fun reading to you," Jakes said.

I said quickly, "I'll be in to tuck you in, sweetie."

"Night, Mommy."

"Thank you. You handled that very well," I said to Jakes when we were alone.

"It wasn't hard. I like her. She's a cutie. And she's smart. Just like her mom." He smiled and I smiled back at him.

We were sitting on the sofa together, one at each end, with a cushion between us.

"What's happening with the new case?" I asked.

"Alex, do you want to talk about Randy—"

"No, I don't," I said. "I've already given that son of a bitch too much of my time. He sent me a note, and I panicked for a moment. My producer is trying to find out how he got onto the lot, and you're going to find him, so no, I don't want to talk about him anymore. Not now."

"Okay," he said. "Okay, Alex. It's your call."

"Tell me what you worked on today."

"I figured something out."

"What?"

"We don't have to solve all the murders," he said.

"Why not?"

"I think it's a mistake to think that way when

they're multiple, or even the work of a serial killer. If we solve one, we solve them all."

"I get it," I said. "Since you think the same person did them all, you only have to solve one to find the . . . murderer."

"Right."

"But . . . which one do you work on?"

"The one that wasn't planned," he said. "The one that looks as if it was a spur-of-the-moment thing and not premeditated."

I stared at him, and then it came to me. "Henri's murder."

"Right."

"What about your partner?" I asked. "And your boss? What do they think of this theory?"

"Len is going to keep working on the murders of the actors," Jakes said. "I'm going to work on the murder of the hairdresser."

"And what do I do?"

"Well," he said, "for one thing we have to keep you out of Captain Carpenter's sight."

"And then?"

"You're going to help me question the people who knew Henri."

"His neighbors?" I asked.

"Yes, them, too," he said, "but I was thinking about his coworkers. Do you know how long he was working on your show?"

"No," I said, "but he was there when I got there."

"So you need to take me to the studio with you."

"Tomorrow's Saturday," I said. "We'll have to wait until Monday."

"Okay, then," he said, "we'll go to his home tomorrow, ask around."

"Wasn't that done already?" I asked. "I mean, you people do a . . . canvass?"

"Yes, some of our patrol guys and some other detective did it," he said. "But I want to do it myself. I need to know all about Henri Marceau."

"But—" I stopped short.

"Come on, Alex," Jakes said. "If you've got something to say, say it."

"What if Henri was just killed by a jealous boyfriend, or something like that?"

"That's too much of a coincidence for me," he said. "Two people connected with your show, killed so close together? And don't forget, Henri said he had something to tell you."

"That's right."

"Maybe he had something to show you, too," Jakes said, "and maybe it's still in his apartment."

"So we'll go and check it out tomorrow?"

"Yes," he said. "I'll pick you up early—that is, unless you had other plans? Something with Sarah?"

"No definite plans," I said. "I just usually spend the day with her. But I'll make it up to her later."

"I'd better go, then," he said. "You have to tuck her in."

I walked him to the door, where he held me and kissed me good night—only it was more than a goodnight kiss.

"I'll see you in the morning, about nine," he said. "Good night."

"Night, Jakes."

Chapter 55

Jakes picked me up at nine o'clock the next morning. As I got in the car he said, "Good morning," and handed me a container of coffee.

"I thought we'd go over to Henri's place first and then stop for breakfast after we've looked around a bit."

"You're the boss," I said. "What I mean is, you're the detective."

He laughed. "I know what you meant, Alex."

We drove mostly in silence. I don't think either of us was fully awake yet.

He parked in front of Henri's building. We left our coffee in the car and walked up the front steps. The door was locked. I looked to him for guidance.

"Just push all the bells," he said. "Somebody will buzz us in."

"It's that easy?"

"Watch."

Between us we pressed all the buzzers, and immediately somebody buzzed the door open.

When we got to Henri's door, though, it was a

different story. It was locked, and there was yellow evidence tape still across the doorway.

"Now what?" I asked.

"You forget," he said. "I'm the detective in charge."

He took a ring of keys from his pocket, found the right one and put it in the lock. One turn and the door was open.

"Follow me," he said. He ducked under the tape that crisscrossed the doorway, and I was careful to do exactly the same thing.

Inside I said, "Hey, detective in change, why are we slipping under the tape?"

"I like to be able to tell if anybody was here," he said. "Anybody inexperienced with the tape would have disturbed it. When we leave, I still want to leave it intact, just in case."

"So you're sure no one's been in here since you and your men left?"

"Reasonably sure, yeah. Place looks like the same mess."

"Okay," I said, "so tell me what we're looking for."

"Same as before," he said, reminding me of our last case together, when we'd broken into someone's home—only I'd gotten hit on the head that time. "You'll know when you see it."

"Okay. I'll start in the kitchen."

"Wait," he said, digging into his jacket pocket. "The lab already went through this place for prints, but wear these anyway." He held out a pair of latex gloves.

"Okay," I said. Pulling them on, I moved into the kitchen.

"I'll start in his bedroom," Jakes said.

I went through the cabinets and drawers and didn't find anything out of place in the kitchen. The counters were covered with the usual—salt and pepper shakers—and canisters were full of the usual—sugar, flour, tea bags.

There were no extravagances in Henri's kitchen. No fancy coffeemakers, no carving machines, blenders, et cetera. The refrigerator was more empty than full—some bad milk, three bottles of Corona, two half-filled bottles of wine (one red, one Chablis), two bottles of Snapple, a couple of plastic containers with leftovers and some Chinese food containers. The lettuce crisper had a half a head of lettuce going brown. What the fridge really needed was a box of baking soda in the back.

In the freezer were a few frozen dinners, an ice cube maker, one of those cold compresses, two pints of ice cream—Rocky Road and Cherry Garcia—both half empty. Nothing hidden in the back. I closed it. It had a water-and-ice dispenser right in the door. You can switch the setting from water to ice and back. At the moment it was set on ice.

I turned around, leaned against the refrigerator and surveyed the room. Had I missed anything? I'd be embarrassed if Jakes walked in and saw something I hadn't.

There was a Georgia O'Keeffe calendar hanging on the wall. Some dates were circled, but there didn't seem to be a pattern. There were too many to be the days of any of the murders. I checked the previous month. More circles, sometimes three and four days in a row, then nothing, and then it would start again. It reminded me of the way some people tracked a diet—circles for the days they stayed on the diet, and no circles when they cheated.

I looked around for an address book. Some people kept them in the bedroom, others in the kitchen. I found recipe books and diet paperbacks. No address book or appointment book.

When I was finally ready to give up on the kitchen, I walked into the living room and found Jakes sitting on the sofa. On the coffee table in front of him was a combination leather address and appointment book. He was leafing through it, but there was a defeated slump to his shoulders.

"You found his address book," I said. "That's good. No, wait. Didn't you say last time we were here that you found an address book?"

"Yeah, we did," he said. "This is another one. I found it in the closet. This one's more involved. It's like a daily planner, with names, addresses, calendar. . . ." He looked up at me. "I was just thinking. . . ."

"Boy, no good news ever came after those words," I said. "About what?"

"My theory about solving one murder," he said. "I may have chosen the wrong one."

"Why?"

"If the same person who killed Masters and the other actors also killed Henri, it was only to shut him up. It was an afterthought. We're not going to find anything here to tell us who it was. If the murder was personal, that's where we'd be likely to find something helpful in an address book or stuffed under a mattress."

"You looked under the mattress?"

He nodded. "And the bed."

"Bathroom?"

"Yeah, everywhere. You know what? The way this place was tossed, it's clear that whoever did it didn't know what they were looking for."

"I see what you mean. They looked in drawers, canisters, under seat cushions."

"They were just trying to get lucky—but let's talk about this book."

I sat down in an armchair. "Henri had something he wanted to tell me or maybe show me. Maybe it was this book. Maybe that's why it was hidden in the closet. Maybe it's what the killer was looking for, too."

I tried to think back. "I'm not sure," I said, "but my point is, he wanted me to come here. There had to be a reason for that."

"Okay," he said, "I'm finished with the bedroom. I'm going to check in here. Why don't you sit tight, go through this book and tell me if you recognize a name?"

"Okay."

I started at the As and began flipping pages. The book was setup for addresses, phone numbers—home and cell—Web sites, e-mail addresses, the works.

"You recognize any names yet?"

"Well, yeah," I said. "A couple of producers from my show and other shows, but he worked there, so that's not unusual."

"Anybody else? Actors?" He put his hand down an empty vase.

"Not yet."

He pulled his hand out of the vase. "How did the kitchen look to you?" he asked.

"How do you mean?"

"Lived in?"

"Pretty much," I said. "Leftovers in the fridge, frozen dinners in the freezer and a marked-up calendar."

"Marked up?"

"Dates circled."

"Any notes? Appointments?"

"Not on the pages I looked at, but I only checked this month and last."

"No doctor appointments?"

"No, why?"

"Lots of medication in the master bathroom," he said.

"The only bathroom," I pointed out.

"Well, there were prescription bottles in there with Henri's name on them."

"And the doctor's name?"

"Different doctor on every bottle."

"That's odd."

"Not if he was working some kind of scam to get drugs," Jakes said. "You go to a doctor and give him symptoms, but symptoms you know fit your phony ailment so that you know what meds he's going to prescribe."

"And you can't do that with the same doctor twice?"

"Not without raising a red flag."

"So Henri was selling drugs? Prescription drugs?"

Jakes shrugged. "Either that or he just liked them. He ever seem high when he was at work?"

"No . . . not that I can remember."

"Maybe he got high at home, then."

I was still leafing through the book, and when I got to the Rs, something jumped out at me.

"Bingo."

"Whaddya got?"

I put my finger on the name and said, "Nate Russell."

"But Nate Russell didn't . . ." Jakes said. "He auditioned but never . . . in here would Ross have . . ."

Chapter 56

Jakes came over and sat next to me. We both stared at Nate's name in the dead man's address book. Then we looked at each other.

"Any others?" he asked.

"Wait."

I had been looking through the book page by page. Now I turned to specific pages that corresponded with the names of all the dead men.

"Here's Jackson Masters," I said. "I missed it. It's under J, not M."

"Any others?"

"No," I said, "Just those two."

"Nate's father said he was gay."

"But Jackson . . ."

"I know," Jakes said. "He was supposedly a stud."

"He could still have been a stud," I said. "Just . . ."

"For the other team."

"Or both."

Jakes sat back, and so did I.

"Well," he said, "it's a connection. He knew Jackson because he worked with him on your soap."

"Right."

"But Nate Russell didn't work on a soap," Jakes said. "He auditioned but never got a part. So how would Henri know him?"

"I just had a thought," I said.

"Do I want to hear it?"

"If you're here with me," I asked, "who's looking for Nate Russell?"

"There *are* other cops working on this, Alex," Jakes said. "We've got an alarm on him, and I've got somebody watching his mother's house."

"Your captain never changed her mind about bringing her in?"

"No—I only would have been able to charge her with obstruction. Let's keep our eye on the ball right here, Alex."

"Sorry," I said. "I was just wondering."

"This connects Henri to Nate," he said, tapping the book.

"Maybe they went to the same bars," I offered. "Maybe Henri was doing hair on the side."

"Yeah, maybe . . ."

He continued to search the living room, but another thought came to me. How did we know the killer didn't find what he was looking for after he killed Henri?

I decided not to ask.

I finished with the book and closed it. The only thing it told us was that Henri knew Nate. We also knew Henri knew Jackson Masters. What we didn't know was if Nate knew Jackson.

I watched Jakes kick at fallen seat cushions and look behind drapes. I watched him skirt a leather ottoman that had been kicked over on its side. In fact, he did it several times.

"Okay," he said finally. "I'm done. Let's take that book with us. We're just going to have to find Nate Russell and sweat him."

"And his mother?"

"Yeah, her, too."

He started over to me and tripped over the fallen ottoman.

"Damn!"

"Wait a minute," I said.

I got up from the sofa and walked to the ottoman. It was brown leather, and was not part of a set. It had been bought separately from the rest of the furniture in the room.

"I've seen this style before," I said, bending over and righting it. "It should have—Yes, there it is." A small leather loop stuck out. We hadn't seen it before because the ottoman had been lying on top of it. I put my finger through the loop and pulled. The side of the ottoman fell open, revealing two drawers.

"Let me guess," Jakes said. "Pottery Barn?"

"Probably QVC," I said. "Let's just hope the killer didn't see it."

I opened the top drawer and it was empty.

"Damn," Jakes said.

I closed it and opened the second drawer. "What's your police word for *bingo*?" I asked.

"Bingo," he said.

I reached into the drawer and came out with a large leather-bound scrapbook.

"Open it," he said.

"Don't you want to?"

"You found it," he said. "I would've missed it if you hadn't been here, Alex. You do the honors."

I opened it.

Chapter 57

It could have been naked photos of the men he'd slept with. It could have been a scrapbook of his favorite baseball teams. It could even have been a collection of his favorite cartoon strips. Or it could have been a stamp collection. But it wasn't.

"A scrapbook of newspaper articles," Jakes said, looking over my shoulder.

It started with pieces about certain TV shows. The clippings were from different papers, including *Variety*. New shows holding auditions, old shows looking for new blood. A red *X* had been marked through some.

"Jakes, this isn't Henri's. This looks like a guy keeping clippings of his failures."

"Keep turning pages," Jakes said. "Let's find out who this belongs to. It's a sure bet that whoever was keeping this book was here looking for it and killed Henri."

I started turning pages quickly until Jakes said, "Whoa, whoa, slow down. Look." He pointed. "Notes in the margin."

The handwriting was cramped. I turned the book

sideways so we could read them. One word leaped out at us.

"Mom?" I said.

"Not only 'Mom,' " Jakes said, pointing to the line that said, *Mom did this!*

"This is Nate Russell's scrapbook," I said. "How did Henri get it?"

"That's a good question," he said. "Come on, let's go."

"Where?"

"Someplace quiet where we can go through this book, inch by inch," he said.

"Don't you have to take this in as evidence?" I asked.

He smiled at me and said, "Eventually, but right now it'll do more good in my hands."

We found a small bar that appeared to be a cigar smokers' club. In fact there was a huge humidor next to the bar. Jakes picked out a table in the back, left me with the book and went to get us some drinks. He came back with a beer bottle and a red wine.

He sat and we continued to peruse Nate Russell's scrapbook. The contents were 100 percent made up of newspaper clippings that had to do with TV auditions—and murders. Each time we found an article on one of our victims, Nate had written something about his mom in black marker.

Mom did this!

This one was Mom's fault.

This looks like Mom.

One even said, *"Oh, Mom,"* with many exclamation points after it.

I turned my head to look at Jakes. "Do you really think Nate believes that his mom could be the killer?"

"From what he's written here, I think he *knows* his mom is the killer."

"Then are you going to arrest her?"

"Not on what I have here, no," he said. "I'd need Nate to make a statement, and even then it would only be his opinion. No, I need evidence before I can arrest her."

"So how do we get evidence?"

"Well, there are a few ways we could go," he said. "We could go back to Henri's neighborhood, see if anyone saw someone fitting the mother's description in the area. Or we could go and show her this book, see if she cracks."

"Oooh," I said, "I like that one."

"Or I could reexamine all the cases, question all the neighbors again about seeing someone like her in the area."

I made a face. "That sounds time-consuming."

He smiled. "That's what detective work is all about," he said. "It's legwork, reports and lots of time eaten up."

"Let's do the second one," I suggested. "It's faster."

"The problem with that is, if she doesn't crack, then we've warned her that we know she's the killer."

"She couldn't be the killer by herself, though," I said. "Hey, did we ever find out if she has another son?"

"Yeah, I did find out," he said. "There's another son, Nick, who is away in Chicago."

"Doing what?"

"We're still trying to find that out," he said.

"O'Hare is a major airport," I said. "He could get here fast if she needed him."

"So you think the mother's not only our killer, but she brought the other son into it?"

"We know she'd need help to do some of the things the killer did," I argued.

"What about Nate?"

"These notations sound to me like they come from someone who's complaining about what his mother did."

Jakes closed the book, picked up his beer and sat back.

"Are you going to take that book in and do whatever you have to do with it as evidence?" I asked.

"That would be the smart thing," he admitted. "I haven't really been doing the smart thing lately, though."

"What else would you do with it, then?"

He shrugged. "Take it home, keep studying it? Put it back? Maybe our killer will come back looking for it, the way we did."

"But the killer already looked for it, and Henri ended up dead."

"That's true," Jakes said. "I'm also going to have to check on this Nick in Chicago. I'll have to check with O'Hare and see if he's taken any flights out here."

He fell silent then. He seemed to want to think about things for a while, so I grabbed my wineglass and sat back, my shoulder almost touching his.

Jakes finally decided he had to go back to Parker Center. That meant I couldn't go with him.

"I have to coordinate with my partner and report to my boss," he said.

"I understand," I said. "She wouldn't like seeing me in your office. Or your presence, I guess."

"It's the weekend," he said. "Spend the rest of it with your daughter. Come on, I'll take you home."

In the car I asked, "What are you going to do with the book?"

"I'll take it with me to my office," he said. "Even after I log it in as evidence, I'll be able to go through it—although it's probably told us all it's going to."

"That Adrienne Russell is a murderer?"

"With somebody's help, maybe her son's. Nate probably knows all the answers."

"So find him, and find the answers, right?"

"Right."

He pulled up in front of my house.

"When am I going to see you?" I asked.

"I don't know," he said. "First I have to convince my boss that a woman who looks like Mrs. Butterworth is a killer, and then I need to find the evidence to legally prove it."

"So in an hour or so?" I smiled.

He smiled back. "Maybe a little longer than that. A couple of days, at least. Let's shoot for Monday."

He kissed me good-bye, and then I kissed him good-bye and got out. He had driven away before I realized I forgot to tell him that Monday night I'd be at the Academy of Television for my taping of "An Evening with the Leading Ladies of Daytime."

Chapter 58

I did as Jakes suggested. I spent the weekend playing with my sweet little girl, under the watchful eye of the man Jakes still had watching her. It was hard to believe that Sarah needed protection from her own father. I'm not sure why, but deep down I clung to the thought that he loved her. Which only made him a bigger puzzle to me.

I went to work on Monday and quickly became consumed with some on-set problems. There was an argument between the director and one of the actors over the way a scene should be played. The actor walked off the set screaming he quit, so production came screeching to a halt. To make a long story even longer . . . I had to tape some scenes from a future episode to make up for the scenes not being taped by previously mentioned pissed-off actor. It happens. Unfortunately, it screwed with my time frame. At the end of taping, I realized I had to be at the Academy in North Hollywood in one hour!

It was too late to go home, so I ran up to wardrobe and asked if I could borrow something for the event. At those kinds of shindigs a nice business suit seemed to be the preferred dress code, so I pulled a tailored blue suit with a somewhat plunging neckline and a little lace ruffle around the neck and cuffs. Conservative with a twist. I put the suit on and did the best I could with my hair in the time I had.

I ran out of the studio, almost breaking a heel, jumped in the Porsche and hurriedly drove to North Hollywood to the Academy of Television Arts and Sciences.

Remembering I hadn't called Jakes, I yelled out, "Call Jakes! Call Jakes!" Nothing happened. "Stupid Bluetooth!" I shouted as I was weaving my way up Highland to get to the 101 to the Valley. Then it dawned on me that the Porsche didn't have Bluetooth. Oops! I'd have to call him once I got there.

I was the last leading lady to arrive, so I ran up to the front of the Academy, making my way through a rather large crowd of fans and industry people.

"Ms. Peterson! Alexis!" Cameras were flashing. People were holding out photos to be autographed. As I took a young guy's Sharpie, poised to sign his autograph book, someone grabbed my arm and led me away. "Sorry!" I yelled to the guy.

The woman holding my arm said, "We're running very late. My name's Sandra, and I'm with the Activities Committee. Could you please pose with the others? Quickly, before the symposium starts!"

"Of course, I'd love to." I was pushed in between Melody Thomas Scott and Susan Lucci. Kim Zimmer was on Susan's other side. A flurry of flashbulbs went off, momentarily blinding me.

"Well, hello, ladies! You all look beautiful. How are you?" I asked.

"Hi, Alex. It's so nice to see you. I love your suit!"

Melody laughed. I looked at her and then at the other two and realized we were all in dark suits. I was right about the dress code.

Kim gave me a big hug. "Al. I can't believe what happened at the Emmys. What's going on with that? Have they found the killer?"

"Yes. Have they found the guy? I heard there were other murders," Susan chimed in.

"You're kidding me. I hadn't heard that," Mel said.

They were all looking at me, but before I had a chance to answer, I heard, "Jesus, I thought you weren't going to make it." My manager, Connie, pushed through the crowd and gave me a big hug.

"Excuse me, ladies," I said to them, and then to Connie, "I missed you."

"I missed you, too. You look good." I think she was tearing up a little. Connie was a little rough around the edges, for sure. Gruff and always slightly disheveled. But she was a softie at heart.

"Now, don't make my makeup run," she snuffled.

"Ms. Peterson. We're about to start. Could you please follow me?" Sandra led the way as the other ladies and I followed her to an area behind the stage. The moderator, Harry Smith, was already speaking to the audience, welcoming them, promising a fun and informative evening. He introduced Susan; she walked out to thunderous applause. The rest of us waited for our names to be called, straightening our skirts, pulling down blouses. I took out a compact and was powdering my upper lip when I happened to glance out at the audience from an opening in the curtain. I stopped in mid-powder.

"Son of a bitch. No way," I muttered to myself. I

couldn't believe it. There he was, sitting right in the middle of all those people. My ex. Randy!

I froze, didn't know what to do. And then I snapped out of it and reached for my cell to call Jakes.

"And from *The Bare and the Brazen*, Alexis Peterson!"

"Shit!" I said too loudly, and dropped the phone. Trying to pick it up, I accidentally kicked it, causing it to land somewhere under a snack table in the corner behind the stage. I went to follow it when Sandra came up behind me.

"Harry Smith just called you. Go!" She not so gently pushed me onto the stage. I sort of stumbled out, blinded by the lights. The audience was clapping as I walked to my seat. I waved to everyone, feeling like I was having an out-of-body experience. Looking around the auditorium, I tried to find Randy again. There he was. About ten rows back with a smirk on his face that made my blood pressure rise. We had a brief moment of eye contact.

"What do you have to say to that, Alexis?" Harry had apparently asked me a question.

I looked at him blankly.

"Would you like me to repeat the question? Daydreaming, are we?"

The audience laughed.

"Sorry?" I said.

"Just wondering how you're enjoying playing two characters."

"Oh, so much fun. Really empowering!" I had no idea what I was saying.

Kim Zimmer was introduced next and everyone stood to applaud. By the time they had taken their seats again, Randy was gone. I blinked and looked around the auditorium.

Had I imagined it? Or was I going to have to deal with Randy when this evening was over?

Chapter 59

The rest of the question-and-answer period was a blur. I guess I answered the questions halfway intelligently. No one complained. When it was over, I made a beeline for the back, looking for my phone. I couldn't find it. Anywhere. I desperately wanted to call Jakes. He was supposed to be locating Randy. Did he know the scumbag was here?

I started to look around for Connie, half expecting Randy to appear. After three years, after he just disappeared with all my money and then after that note and the phone call, I didn't know what I'd say or do. I hoped I'd have control and the good sense to not cause a scene in front of my colleagues and fans, but the truth was, I wasn't sure.

"Al."

I turned, wide-eyed, but it was Connie.

"Whoa, Al," she said. "Are you all right?"

"Connie," I said low and urgently, "he's here. Randy's here. I saw him in the audience."

"Are you sure?"

"Positive. Well, sort of."

"Are you positive or not?"

"Yeah, I am. I mean, it was a shock. But it had to be him. Let me have your phone."

"That bastard!" she hissed, and handed me her cell.

"Where's yours?"

I waved her off as I tried to call Jakes. "Shit! No reception in here. I have to get out of here—I need to get to Sarah!"

"People were invited up to talk to you, Al. You're supposed to sign autographs and schmooze a little."

I looked around me. Fans were coming up from the audience, and I didn't see Randy anywhere. Could I trust my eyes? Should I start to doubt myself?

"Did you drive?" she asked.

"Yes; I'm parked on level Two West," I said, still looking out for Randy and handing her back her phone.

"So am I. Take a few photos, sign a couple of autographs and then leave. I'll pick you up right outside the front doors. We'll get your car later."

"Won't that seem too . . . rude?"

"Don't worry," she said. "I'll tell them you had a family emergency."

"Okay. Thanks!" I could always count on Connie.

I was still nervously looking around the room for Randy when someone touched my elbow. Luckily I managed not to jump out of my skin. It was Sandra. She wanted me to stand with the other ladies and meet and greet.

"I'll see you out there," Connie said.

I nodded. She left to go to the parking structure. Connie knew Randy and didn't like him one bit. I hoped she wouldn't run into him. There was no telling what she might do, especially if she was behind the wheel.

As it turned out, it wasn't Randy I had to worry about.

I managed to get away after only a few minutes of signing autographs. I wasn't sure my colleagues would understand and not take offense that I hadn't said good-bye to each of them in turn, but simply waved to everyone and took off.

I tried to keep from running until I got clear of the auditorium. By the time I got to the lobby, I was jogging and bolted through the front doors. No Connie. Shit! I thought. Where was she? I flung off my heels and sprinted to the parking structure. Impatiently I kept pushing the button for the elevator, even though I knew it wouldn't do any good. Once you push it once, it's pushed. Damn it!

When the elevator came, I rushed in and pushed the button P2 West. It lit up but still I kept pushing. I had managed to get a spot right near the elevator, so when the door opened I expected to see my car.

But I was wrong.

"Hi, babe," Randy said, a big smile on the handsome face that used to make me weak in the knees. Now it made my stomach flip in an entirely different way.

"Randy."

"We need to talk."

"I don't want to talk to you," I said, stepping out of the elevator.

"I want to see Sarah."

"You're not seeing Sarah, Randy. Not just like that, out of the blue. Not after three years. It'll mess with her head. What are you trying to do to her? Are you staying? Going to court? Going to jail?" My voice was rising along with my anger. "What the hell are your intentions?"

At that moment I heard someone running, and then I saw Connie hurrying from the other direction.

"Alex!"

Randy turned when he heard my name, and he saw Connie, too. "Oh, hell, are you still workin' with that crazy bitch?"

I didn't understand why Connie was running until we heard the sound of a car screeching. A dark SUV came up from behind and pulled alongside her. The passenger-side door opened and a dark-haired man got out.

"Oh, God," I said. The woman behind the wheel was Adrienne Russell. The man was Nate. He grabbed Connie and started forcing her into the car. She fought him.

"Connie!" I shouted.

"Alex!" Connie called back. At that point Nate punched her on the jaw and pushed her into the car.

"Oh God, oh God, Con," I said.

"Alex—what the hell is going on? Who are those people?" Randy said.

"Get out of my way, Randy!"

Adrienne looked over at me and smiled, nothing like Mrs. Butterworth now.

"Damn it, Randy—"

I tried to go around him, but he stepped into my path. "Alex—" he said again.

And that's when I hit him.

Chapter 60

I felt the shock of the blow all the way up my arm, fearing I might have broken my hand. But as he fell I couldn't spend one minute enjoying his pain. I ran for the Porsche, hoping I could get out of the parking structure in time to see which way Adrienne and Nate had taken Connie.

I dropped my keys the first time I tried to unlock the door. The second time I was more successful. I fitted the key into the ignition and got Marilyn roaring. As I pulled out I saw Randy get up, and then he had to jump out of my way.

Screeching down to the exit, I had to stop and pay at the gate before I could get out. Apparently Adrienne had also stopped to pay. I didn't see the humor until later. Who stops to pay when they're in the middle of a kidnapping?

I couldn't figure out why they would want Connie. Or what they were doing there in the first place.

I drove out of the garage and onto the street, wondering which way to go. I needn't have wondered. Adrienne's SUV was there, parked with the motor running. I didn't know what to do. Get out and ap-

proach it? Call Jakes? Or 911? I didn't have my fucking phone!

The SUV suddenly revved its engine and took off.
I hit the gas and followed. There was no way they
could outrun Marilyn.

Adrienne jumped on the 5 North heading out deep
into the Valley. It was fairly late, and the freeway was
empty enough to allow Adrienne to maintain a speed
upward of eighty miles an hour. It was a speed I could
easily do with the Porsche.

I followed, realizing they were going into a heavily industrialized area. The boonies. No 7-Elevens. No
gas stations. No police stations. Nothing. Finally they
pulled into what looked like a self-storage facility.
They pulled up to the front gate and stopped.

The vehicle idled there, with hardly any movement inside. I stopped several car lengths behind
them, waiting. None of the murders had been committed with a gun, but that didn't mean they didn't
have one.

Suddenly Adrienne's arm came out the window,
and she punched in a code. The gate rolled back
slowly.

I put the Porsche in drive and drove forward
through the rolling gate before it could close.

Chapter 61

Somehow, once we got through the gate, they disappeared.

I stopped the car but kept the motor running and the doors locked. I was hoping to see an address, but it was dark. My headlights shone on a bunch of orange corrugated doors.

I knew I had to get out of the car. I didn't have a flashlight, but I did have a crowbar in the backseat that I kept on the floor for road rage emergencies. I grabbed it, held it tight and got out.

The ground was gravel. My feet crunched as I stepped out. Abruptly I heard other footsteps crunching, as if someone was running up behind me. Before I could move or bring the crowbar up, an arm came around me right under my chin.

"Drop it!" someone said in my ear.

I considered trying to hit whomever it was, but the person tightened his hold and cut off my air. I let the crowbar drop.

The arm released me, and Nate forced me around and pushed me against the car.

He was not a large or imposing person, but I had

the feeling his looks were deceiving. He was definitely stronger than I was, and I didn't think I could sucker punch him the way I had Randy. My hand was still throbbing from that episode.

He pushed me ahead and directed me where to turn. Suddenly there were lights ahead. When we reached the storage units, I saw that one of the doors was open and the interior of one of the larger units was well lit. So well lit that naked bulbs hanging from the ceiling made me squint. But I could still see Connie, tied and gagged and lying on the floor in a corner. Standing near her was Adrienne Russell. Mother and son had dressed alike for their little family outing—sweatshirts, jeans and tennis shoes.

The storage unit looked like a shrine. There were photos of Nate, some furniture, clippings stuck to the walls and boxes, but when I looked closer I could see that the head shots were not of Nate but of someone who looked very much like him.

"That's Nick," Adrienne said. "My other son. Nate's twin, actually."

Adrienne looked bulky in her clothes. Gone were the bun and granny glasses and the Mrs. Butterworth demeanor. There was a shine in her eyes, though, a look I had tried to cultivate when I had once played a slightly mad character in a movie of the week years back, only Adrienne was much more convincing.

"Nick," I said, "your son—the one in Chicago?"

"Your information is old, Alex," Adrienne said. "Yes, Nick went away to do repertory theater—after he had failed at acting in Hollywood. After 'the business' had successfully beaten him down. But they didn't appreciate him there either, so he ended up working odd jobs, embarrassed to tell us. Finally the

despair overtook him so much that he committed sui-
cide. Hanged himself. That sound familiar?"

So Nate had a twin who killed himself because he
couldn't make it as an actor? More likely he took his
life because of a weakness of character, but I didn't
try that suggestion on his grieving mother. I didn't
think she would have appreciated my point of view.
And the hanging thing. That was why she was killing
actors by hanging or strangling them.

I looked around and noticed two things. One: she
was in charge and her son was obviously completely
subservient to her. And two: neither one was holding
a gun. In fact, I didn't see a weapon anywhere, but I
knew that could change in an instant.

"I assume you called Detective Jakes," she said, "so
he's probably on his way here. We'll see how quickly
we can complete our business. We *are* in the middle of
nowhere. It'll take him a while."

I didn't want to let on that it was just me there. No
Jakes.

"Is this the same business you didn't finish that
night on PCH, Adrienne? When you tried to run me
off the road?" I asked, my throat dry. I was glad my
voice hadn't cracked.

She looked at me blankly. "I have no idea what
you're talking about."

"Don't lie, Adrienne. You tried to kill me. Or rather,
Nate did."

"What the hell are you talking about? Don't try to
confuse me! You're so clever, aren't you? With your
words. Your disguises! But you're not so smart. See,
I knew you looked familiar when you and Detective
Jakes came to talk to me, but it wasn't until I read in
the paper that you were going to be at the Academy

tonight that it clicked in my head. The article mentioned how you were playing twins on your show, wearing makeup to alter your appearance. That's when I put it together. And that's when I decided that tonight was the night to get you out of the way."

"Out of the way?" I asked.

"You're in the way of what we're doing for Nick."

"Which is?"

"Removing the competition."

"Nick's dead, Adrienne," I reminded her. "How does killing actors do anything for him now?"

"For his memory!" she shouted. "This is all for him."

"What about Nate?" I asked. "He's still alive. What about his career? He's still auditioning, isn't he?"

"Auditioning." She spat the word out. "Nate is a joke. He never had Nick's talent."

I looked at Nate, but he was staring at the floor, miserable. Then he shouted at her, "Nick never got a good part either, Mom!"

"Shut up! He would have! He needed to keep working at it. It would have happened for him in time!"

I understood. Nick was her pet, her favorite. Nate was the afterthought, the second fiddle. Maybe I could use this little chink in their armor to my advantage.

I looked over. Poor Connie. She had duct tape over her mouth, and her eyes were wide with fright.

If I hadn't known better, I would have thought the pair just seemed like a sad mother-and-son act. Adrienne looked like an old worn-out housewife, dressed for spring cleaning. Nate, slender and unimposing, looked like a kid who wished he were somewhere else.

But they had already killed four or five young men?

I'd lost count. Had they killed Henri? And they were probably planning the same for Connie and me.

Why was I not more frightened? I wondered. Stalling, I said, "Adrienne, I don't know why you took Connie. She has nothing to do with this!"

"I knew you'd follow her. Your faithful manager. Ha! She's your lapdog!" she scoffed. Connie took offense to that and was harrumphing under her taped mouth. "I know how you industry people are. You think you're so much more important than anyone else. So special. So fabulous. You both need to be taught a lesson. A lesson in humility."

I looked around for something to use as a weapon as Adrienne continued with her tirade. I could see childhood things in the unit: toys, games. It seemed she had kept everything Nick ever owned. And then, off to one side, I saw a hockey stick leaning against a box.

"What was it about Nick?" I asked, trying to keep her occupied. I pointed to a photo taped to the metal wall of the unit. "What was different about him? Was he better looking.than Nate?"

"I always knew he was," Adrienne said. "They were identical twins, but I could see a difference." She was staring at the photos of Nick with a frenzied look in her eyes. "See the slight widow's peak on Nick's forehead? The cleft chin? Nate doesn't have that. He's more . . . average. Nick had movie-star good looks. He was destined for greatness. Ahhh!" She choked back tears. "And he was better. At everything. Better at sports, better at school and a superior actor. He could play anything. If he'd only had the chance."

I looked at Nate. His head was down but his eyes were glaring at his mother with what? Stifled rage?

"You have quite a shrine here," I said, moving toward the photos. And the hockey stick. I pointed to some of the photos on the wall. "How do you feel about this, Nate?"

Nate looked up, surprised that someone had spoken to him.

"What do you think of this shrine?"

Connie watched me. There was no way I could communicate anything to her with my eyes, but hopefully she knew I would try to do *something*. If I didn't, we'd be dead.

The hockey stick was near Nate. I hoped it simply looked like I was approaching him and the photos. Adrienne was the biggest threat because she was in charge, but Nate was younger. He was the biggest physical threat to us. After all, he'd slugged Connie and tossed her into the vehicle.

I kept inching toward him.

I needed that hockey stick.

Chapter 62

"Nate loved his brother!" Adrienne said.

"I'll bet he did, in the beginning," I said. "But I know what kind of resentment can build up between siblings when one is favored. Right, Nate?"

Nate looked at me and then at his mother but quickly turned his eyes downward. I moved closer to him.

"He understands what we have to do. For Nick's sake."

It was quiet then. I didn't know if I should make a move or what.

"No, Mom, I don't understand."

Adrienne's head whipped around as if she had never heard this son speak before.

"What did you say?" she spat.

It seemed that Nate having a neutral witness gave him some backbone. "I've never understood. Why him and not me? Maybe if you had given me more attention, I could have been better at things, Mom. It was always Nick does this and Nick does that better. Nick . . . Nick . . . Nick!"

Connie was still watching me, breathing heavily

through her nose, which, thankfully, had not been covered by the tape.

I still didn't feel I could snatch up the hockey stick in one move. Closer . . .

Then something occurred to me. "So Nate, tell us why you kept that scrapbook of all the murders, along with notes about your mother."

"Scrapbook?" Adrienne's head snapped back to me. "What scrapbook?"

Nate tossed me a look of betrayal and his mother one of pure fear. He started to shake his head. Obviously when she had searched Henri's apartment she hadn't known what she was searching for. She must have just been looking to see if there was anything there that could have led to Nate.

"The one Jakes and I found in Henri Marceau's apartment," I said. "You remember Henri, Adrienne? The hairdresser you killed?"

"That sexual deviate?" she screamed, spittle flying from her mouth.

Just what I thought—a hot button.

"How did Henri end up with it, Nate?" I asked. "Were you and he good friends? Was he your lover?"

"Shut up, bitch!" Adrienne yelled at me. She'd stopped looking at Nate and was coming toward me.

"You should see it, Adrienne. Lots of pictures and special notes in red ink, all over the margins. *Mom did it* or *This was Mom's fault,*" I said, thinking on my feet, egging her on.

"My fault?" Adrienne turned to Nate and screamed, "Anything good that you ever had, *I gave you!*"

"No, Mother! You took everything *away* from me, everything I loved!"

"You and that hairdresser? Nick never would have

done anything that disgusting!" All of her attention was on Nate. Now that was all I needed.

I leaped for the hockey stick, wrapped both hands around it and swung. I wanted to hit Adrienne, but Nate was the closest and most logical target. I felt the impact to his head, and a pain so horrible went running up from my hand all the way to my arm.

"Bitch!" Adrienne screamed.

I turned quickly, holding the stick ready, but she had dashed to the other wall, grabbed her purse and come out with a silver gun. Damn it! A hockey stick against a gun . . . and suddenly I was thinking about Sarah.

"No!" I shouted. I dropped the stick, but before I could move, Connie rolled over and bowled Adrienne's feet out from under her. She fell heavily on top of Connie, the gun skittering across the floor toward me. Even before it stopped I slapped it with the hockey stick. A perfect shot! It went flying out the door into the night . . . right past Jakes!

He stood in the doorway of the unit, gun in hand, and then moved quickly, pulling Adrienne off Connie and yanking her to her feet.

Nate was on the floor, bleeding from the head.

I ran to Connie, rolled her over and pulled the tape from her mouth. "Are you all right?"

She spat and then yelled, "That crazy old bitch! I think she broke my arm!"

I looked at Jakes, who said to me flatly, "I can't leave you alone for a minute, can I?"

Chapter 63

It was like a scene out of a movie—or a soap opera.

I was sitting on the back of an ambulance while an EMT bandaged my hand. He was pretty sure I had broken one or two fingers when I punched Randy. An X-ray would confirm it. I had spoken to the police and made sure Sarah was safe at home and asleep in her bed.

They had taken Adrienne away. Another EMT was bandaging Nate's head before the police would take him away. I couldn't see where Connie was, but she was being cared for, too.

Jakes came over to me and put his hand on my shoulder. The EMT walked away.

"How did you know where I was?" I asked, shaking. "I couldn't call you because I lost my phone." I think I was in shock.

"I finally located Randy just in time to follow him to the Academy. I saw him meet with you and then saw Connie get snatched. As you jumped into your Porsche to go and save the day, I had to decide to either get Randy or follow you. I chose you." He turned me around to face me and put his arms around me.

"Thank God you did," I said. "My hero cop."

"Me? You're the hero, tearing off after them like that, knocking your ex on his ass. Then following those two in here, arming yourself with a hockey stick. Against a gun." He was saying all this while rubbing my back. He smelled like Obsession.

"Yeah, what was she doing with a gun?" I asked. "She'd never used one on a victim before."

"Who knows? Maybe she was planning to use it on you."

"If she'd been holding it the whole time, I never would have been able to grab that stick—"

"But she wasn't. You saved the day, Alex," he said again. "You're quite a hero."

I put my face up to his. We kissed and I melted into it. God, I wished we were somewhere else now—anywhere!

He held my face in his hands. "I was worried about you. Scared shitless, actually."

"Really? I guess we worry about each other a lot. Don't we?" I said matter-of-factly. "But I don't think we have to worry about your captain. You've got me as a witness and Connie, too. She heard everything."

"Connie's on her way to the hospital to be checked out. I'll interview her later."

"Poor Connie! She was so afraid! I mean, so was I. Hearing Adrienne going on about her son. She's nuts, you know? Completely insane!"

"Did Adrienne actually say she and Nate murdered our victims?" he asked.

"Yes, she did," I said.

"So then your friend, Jackson, didn't have a connection to Henri except as a coworker. It was Nate who got Henri killed."

"Oh, God!" I said, suddenly.

"What?"

"Adrienne also said she had nothing to do with trying to run me off of PCH. After everything else she told me, I don't know why she'd lie about that."

"So that leaves Randy." This seemed to disturb him.

"Wait a minute. If you followed me, who nabbed Randy?"

He hesitated before saying, "No one. I, uh, lost you as we got to this area, which is why I was a little late. I put everyone on you. When I saw this place, I decided to check it out, and when I saw your car I started checking units."

"That means Randy's still out there." I didn't like the way that sounded. Or the way it made me feel.

He seemed to know exactly what I was thinking. "Don't worry. You've got me." He held me tightly in his arms. With all the craziness going on around us, our hugging made no sense at all. But I felt safe. I held on to him until every part of my body was touching every part of his.

"Looks like we've got each other."

Turn the page
for a sneak peek at
another Soap Opera Mystery
by Eileen Davidson

DIVA LAS VEGAS

Available now from Obsidian.

"Honey, that girl is butt naked!"

"No, she's not."

"Alex! She's naked and so is the girl next to her. Look right there." He pointed to a particular area of her body.

I took a step closer, looking in the general direction of where his finger was pointing and trying to be as discreet as possible.

"*Eww!* Oh my God, George." I gasped, turning away. "You're so right! She is naked." I couldn't believe what I was seeing. So I looked again, just to make sure. At first glance the girl looked like she was wearing a tuxedo, complete with black tie and tails. And the girl next to her appeared to be dressed like a mermaid. Sparkles and scales everywhere. And I do mean everywhere. But it was paint. Meticulously applied and not a detail missed.

As I took another peek, I winced.

"How did they get the paint right there? Awkward."

Talk about an assault to the senses. We had just stepped out of the limo and into the most flamboyant, intense party in the world. We were at the infamous Playboy Mansion. I hadn't been here since I was in my early twenties. The main house was a "traditional" Tudor-style mansion. But tonight was the annual Halloween bash. Tombstones lay scattered across the sprawling lawn and bodies squirmed to free themselves from their graves. There were cobwebs hanging from the windows and doors. Giant ghouls and ghosts (people on stilts) walked the grounds, chasing half-naked women.

In front of the mansion by the driveway was a large haunted house Hugh Hefner set up every year. A line of about forty people waited to get in. I've heard it takes a good week to put together but is well worth the wait. Everyone I had talked to said it was the most frightening haunted house they'd ever experienced. I was trying to take it all in when I heard my name.

"Hey, Alex! Nice outfit!" she said, sarcastically.

"Hi, Shana. I know, I know. I ordered it online. Not exactly like the picture."

I knew I had to get sexy for Hef's party, so I had found this Little Bo Peep outfit. It seemed like a good idea at the time. How was I supposed to know there'd be so many ruffles? I didn't feel particularly sexy with a pile of blonde ringlets on my head and the big blue bow on my butt, not to mention petticoats jutting out and knocking everything over in my path. I was carrying a staff, just to finish off the look. George thought it would be funny if he went as a sheep. Get it? Little Bo Peep has lost her sheep? I wasn't thrilled with the idea but George had really pushed for it. He's my best friend and hairdresser—he's brilliant at both. Although sometimes his idea of what is funny can be a little questionable.

First of all, he's only five feet four inches tall and when not on a diet tends to lean a little toward chubby. He had on a full-body sheep costume complete with a headpiece tied under his chin. It was made of faux fur that was white and tightly curled. His nose was even painted black. He looked like Richard Simmons on acid. He looked like a cotton ball that had been shoved into a light socket. He looked like he was the crazy, gone-wrong entertainment at a kids' party. He looked like . . . oh, you get it.

Shana Stern, on the other hand, was an old pro. An ex-Playmate, she obviously had been to the mansion many, many times. She was wearing a barely there devil outfit. So were about fifty other women. Bobbing up and down across the lawn was a sea of devil horns. I didn't personally know any devils who wore thongs but apparently they do at Hef's parties. Shana was pushing forty but, God bless her, she could still pull it off. Tasteful? I'm not so sure. You know that saying? Just because you can doesn't mean you should!

"Well, I'm glad you guys could make it! And George, you've outdone yourself. But couldn't you have toned it down a bit? Look around! There aren't a lot of gay guys here. At least none that are out of the closet."

"Honey, this place has seen it all but they've never seen the likes of me. I figured go big or go home. *Baaa!*"

"Thanks for inviting us, Shana. This'll be fun."

Shana was the newest cast member on my show, *The Bare and the Brazen.* She hadn't been on the show that long but we had become friends despite our personality differences. She had a bit of an inner diva but I liked her anyway. She had a sweet side to her too.

"Let's go get hammered!" Shana said. She grabbed my hand and I grabbed George's, uh, hoof and off we went.

As we entered the massive foyer, we saw every kind of costume imaginable. Most of the women were in angel, devil, maid or fairy costumes. Sexy was the name of the game and there was no shortage of bare flesh, even if originality was lacking.

Shana dragged me outside to the backyard, which was the size of a football field. It was covered completely by a massive tent.

"Ow! Watch where you're going!"

"Sorry!" My stiff crinoline had taken out some guy, but it wasn't just any guy; it was actor Matthew Perry. And he was chatting with talk-show guy Bill Maher. Neither looked at each other while they talked. More like scoping out the hundreds of women. I couldn't fault them, though. This place was very distracting, with a four-to-one ratio of women to men. *Naked* women to *clothed* men.

Music pounded from the multitude of speakers. Four girls dressed only in body paint were dancing on the stage in cages.

"Oh my God! That's Paris Hilton!" George gasped. I turned and, sure enough, Paris had jumped up on the stage and was doing an impromptu cage dance.

"Wow, she looks . . . cute." In a fairy costume. Of course.

Just as we were approaching one of five bars on the premises, we heard, "Miss Stern? Miss Stern?" A man pushed a beautifully wrapped gift basket into Shana's arms.

"Oh, sweet Jesus! Not you again. Security!" Shana yelled. Loudly.

"Wait! Miss Stern! I just wanted a photo with you. Please. One photo." He held up his camera phone. Real cameras were strictly banned from Hef's parties.

"What's the matter, Shana?" I asked.

"This guy's a stalker. I've been getting ten letters from him a week for the last two years. He's not supposed to be anywhere near me!" As she spoke she put me in between her and the man. Having had my own share of psycho stalkers, I was nervous, so I grabbed George and used him as a buffer.

"Hey, missy . . . I know what you're do—" Before George could finish his sentence, two extremely buff security guards jogged up.

"Sorry, Miss Stern. We don't know how he got in!" the tall blonde one said.

"But that's your job, isn't it?" she berated them. "Aren't you supposed to know these things? Aren't you called 'security' exactly for that reason?" I understood that Shana was upset, but it seemed to me she was coming down on these guys a little too hard.

"Perhaps they should call you 'morons.' Would that be more appropriate?" The security guards didn't look too happy, especially since people had started to gather around. It was embarrassing.

"I'm really sorry, Miss Stern. I just wanted one photo. I'm harmless—I swear." The stalker was still trying to take a photo of her even as he was being led away.

"There are so many weirdoes in the world and too many idiots. Now I really need a drink!" Shana said as she dumped the gift basket into the closest trash bin.

"Three shots of tequila, with salt and lime. Make mine a double. And don't take too long!" Shana shouted to the bartender. He gave her a look that would have stopped most people cold. Her inner diva wasn't so inner anymore. It had reared its ugly head. I turned around to face her.

"Hey, I know the stalker thing can be upsetting, but you don't have to be so rude. And a double? Isn't that a little hard-core?" I asked quietly.

I finally got a good look at her and could see from her demeanor this wasn't the first shot she'd ordered tonight.

Shana ignored me. "Hey, George." She was suddenly slurring. "Could you pleashe go and check out the grotto? It'sh over there behind the buffet. That'sh where everyone usually ends up naked at around three ay em. See if anyone is starting early, huh?"

George looked at me with a raised eyebrow, knowing he was being brushed off. I shrugged, not knowing what was up with her.

"Sure, honey. I'll be right back. Save me that shot."

George and I exchanged a glance and off he went, wagging his tail behind him.

"What's going on with you?" I asked her. The bartender set down the three shots and Shana tossed back her double without hesitation. The movement caused her to stagger.

"Whoa, take it easy." I put my arm around her. "Are you okay?"

"You have no idea what it'sh like, Alex. No idea. I can't talk to anyone. And I mean anyone. You think I asked you here just as a friendly invitation?" She brushed away a strand of bleached blonde hair that had gotten stuck in her lip gloss. "I've got a big problem. I didn't know who elshe to talk to. At work, umm, you seem nice. You know, normal?" Now that might be a stretch, but I guess everything is relative.

"Well, sure, Shana. If you're having a problem, I'm happy to talk to you. Is it about that stalker? I do have some experience dealing with guys like him."

"No! It'sh not about that stupid jerk." She spit the *J* in my face. I flinched. "Just listen. I know your boyfriend is a cop, right?" She was referring to Detective Frank Jakes. Boyfriend always sounds strange at this stage of life but he was a boy and he was my friend. Oh, whatever.

"Yeah, he's a detective with the LAPD. Why? Are you in legal trouble?"

"It's more than that. Much more." She was really nervous and kept looking over her shoulder, sucking on her lower lip.

"Okay, soooo—" But before she could answer, a very tall wood nymph interrupted us. I guess she was a wood nymph. She had leaves strategically placed on her green-painted body and a head covered in leaves and flowers. Maybe she was a tree branch. Or a green tomato worm.

"Shana! There's a photographer taking pictures of all the Playmates from the eighties in the dining room. You were Miss September 1986. We need you!"

"Oh, for chrissakes. Just do it without me, can't you? I'm busy!" Shana snapped. "I'm talkin' to someone."

"You don't have to be so mean." Wood Nymph seemed hurt, and yet I got the impression she was used to this side of Shana.

"We need you. We have all the girls from 'eighty-six but you. Except one. It's important to Hef."

"Like Hef could give a shit!" Shana clearly didn't want to go but "duty" called. She took George's shot and tossed it down the hatch. Geez, she could drink. But could she stand?

"I'll be right back and I'll tell you . . . everything." She had a crazed look in her eyes. She pointed her finger at me and again said, "I'll be right back! Twenty minutes or so. Okay? Right back."

She took her fingers and plumped up her teased hair, licked her lips and put on a well-worn Playmate pout. She and Wood Nymph made their way through the crowd on their wobbly stilettos, heading back toward the mansion. I didn't know then that Shana's fanny, covered in red fishnet pantyhose, would be the last I'd ever see of her . . . alive.